For Susan –
I Hope you
enjoy the Oro
story

Oro,
The "Tail" Continues

Ray "Grizzly" Racobs 4/24/11

Ray "Grizzly" Racobs

OSO ORO

WingSpan Press

Printed in the United States of America

Published by WingSpan Press, Livermore, CA
www.wingspanpress.com

The WingSpan name, logo and colophon are the trademarks of
WingSpan Publishing.

ISBN 978-1-59594-175-6

First edition 2007

Library of Congress Control Number 2007930006

ACKNOWLEDGMENTS

I thank my family members (Mom), all my friends (both of you), my co-workers (especially Linda Wullschleger) and the many known and unknown folks out there for their support in purchasing my first two books.

I am grateful to Haysville Community Library's Head Librarian Betty Cattrell and the members of Friends of the Library for their help with book signings and promotions and don't worry FOL President Lyn Worrell; I'll keep the tradition alive and hold copy #1 of Oro's first sequel for you.

I thank C.J. Cross, former owner of the *Haysville Times,* for giving me the chance to work as a freelance reporter and columnist with her paper. The experience has helped to make me a better writer.

I want to express my appreciation to the members of Kansas Author's Club and Kansas Writer's Association for the work they do in helping novice and experienced writers improve their craft.

Every writer should consider meeting with a critique group and the one I frequented, headed by the talented author Gordon Kessler, was enjoyable, as well as being informative and helpful.

The worst part of writing anything is the proof reading and I thank my mother, Virginia Racobs and two college students, Bridget Hogan and Katie Young, for their help in that process. For the price of a dinner and a book their services were a great deal.

Promotional materials are a must for any sales campaign and Susie Colbert of City Blue Print, Inc., Wichita, KS, has been instrumental in helping me plan and produce book markers, business cards, flyers and thank you notes. She also displays my books on the premises for sale.

And with the cliché "last, but certainly not least" I thank Lynda, my wife, who has quietly (usually) and patiently (usually) waited through many a postponed (usually) date night, because I was writing something for a deadline somewhere. When my Oro series becomes a best seller on someone's list, a major motion picture and a television series, her indulgencies will have paid off.

If, for some reason, you were left off the acknowledgement list, I thank you, too and sincerely apologize for the oversight. Let me know and I'll correct the error in my next book, *Oro: Canine Versus Crime.*

TABLE OF CONTENTS

INTRODUCTION

THOSE OF US with pets have all done it; we have talked to them. How cool would it be if they could respond?

My lovely and loving wife, Lynda and I were relaxing in lawn chairs on the bank of Rainbow Lake, while vacationing in an area west of Gunnison, Colorado. Oso Oro, my golden retriever/great Dane mix, sat between us. Lynda read, while her sheltie, Cricket, lay in her lap; asleep.

Our little group occupied a spot at the edge of a grove of aspens on a delightfully cool August afternoon. I was trying to concentrate on writing another chapter for my first book, *Grizzly's This 'N That* (Author House, Dec '04). Grizzly is a nickname I picked up a few years back and the book deals with an assortment of anecdotes, old proverbs and quotes. Little was being accomplished on this fine day, because the glorious scenery of the clear, glass-like water, back dropped by a stand of timber on a mountain slope, competed for my attention.

Oso Oro, (translates to "gold bear" in Spanish) looked with such intensity at the landscape before us that I wondered what he was thinking. I verbalized my thoughts with, "Oso, what is going on in that brain of yours?" He only answered with a wag of his tail and a lick to my hand.

It was at that point in time when *Oro, The Incredible Dog* (Publish America, July '05) came to life. The idea of how great it would be to communicate with my canine friend was not new, but at that moment I was compelled to act on the thought. Finishing *Grizzly's This 'N That* became a difficult task, for I was almost consumed with writing about the unique dog.

Right after I began the novel, I knew I would write a

sequel and *Oro, The "Tail" Continues* was simply waiting for its turn. And not long after I began to write the sequel I realized I would continue with a third ... and so on. I hope you enjoy the continued exploits of Oro.

CHAPTER 1

PAST REFLECTIONS

MY TIME AT home on the old farm place, called Rainbow Acres, was one of total contentment. Oro, my faithful and almost constant companion and I were having a pleasant conversation ... of sorts. The vocal part of our communication, however, was totally one sided. To an observer, Oro would appear to be merely listening, since he wasn't speaking.

He is like the brother or even the son I never had and may know me better than Lea, my lovely fiancée, but that's OK. And it's OK that he isn't even human, because he's a unique golden retriever and Great Dane mix. "Oh, just a dog," you might say ... "man's best friend," but Oro is a hundred times or more as special as any ordinary canine. Remember, I said he was unique.

Oro has the ability to not only understand all human speech, but is also able to read all human thought. When our paths crossed last summer in Colorado, I was, to say the least, startled when I learned of Oro's ability, but he was equally amazed to find that I was able to receive his thoughts, as if he had spoken them to me. As it turned out, I was the only human Oro had ever been able to communicate with.

Before I ramble on too far, I should give you some background info about myself and the "tail" behind Oro (pun intended). I'm Will Jacobs and I used to teach American history at the high school level. I took a year's leave of absence from teaching after a spectacular stroke of luck. I won the jackpot in Kansas' multi-state lottery and collected, after taxes, the enormous sum of thirty-two million dollars, plus a good amount of change, over a hundred grand, which in itself would have tickled me almost to death.

After eliminating all of my own indebtedness, I invested the bulk of the proceeds, financially assisted all my known relatives and spoiled myself some (OK, maybe a lot). For my impending vacation, I decided to purchase a motor home and a Jeep Wrangler to pull behind it. This fact brings Lea (pronounced like "Lee") into the picture. I asked her to help me select the vehicles, but there were other motives behind the request, for I wanted her to join me on the trip. Lea's acceptance of my offer positively changed my life then, now and will into the future. I knew she was special, but our time spent together in Colorado only strengthened my feelings for her and the relationship between us.

I met Lea after she replaced the retiring freshman English teacher, where I taught. Lea and I developed a good friendship and occasionally dated during the school year. Even though my feelings for her were quite strong, I took no major initiative to advance our relationship any further than being very good friends. At the time, I was ashamed of where I lived and of my financial situation. Both conditions were the result of an ugly and costly divorce.

Lea's intellect, beauty and sophistication (not necessarily in that particular order) often made me feel uncomfortable, but my previous low self-esteem and monetary status had now drastically changed. The improvement seemed to coincide with the day I won the lottery. Imagine that!

Obtaining Oro was another bit of good luck. Lea and I met Darcie while "camping out" in the motor home north of Durango, Colorado. She was a senior at Oklahoma State University in Stillwater and Oro's owner. Circumstances in her life prevented her from keeping her pet. Her problem led to my fortunate acquisition of the incredible dog. Oro was sad to part company with Darcie, but was also excited about the change, for he saw ways to productively utilize his ability. With Darcie, he was never able to act upon situations that presented themselves to him. For Oro, the ability to hear and understand people's thoughts had been more like a curse, but with me he now felt that his "sixth sense" was truly a gift.

Not long after our Colorado trip, I bought a spectacular, but old farmstead place near Wichita, Kansas. Lea, Oro and I decided to call the 160 acre property Rainbow Acres. The name was in honor of Rainbow Lake, a beautiful area near Black Mesa Reservoir, west of Gunnison, Colorado. All three of us loved the spot.

After acquiring the splendid two-and-a-half story farmhouse, I asked Lea for her hand in marriage. Thankfully, she accepted. Good things, it's been said, come in three's and my share was complete after winning the lottery, finding Oro and having Lea accept my proposal. If it is all a dream, then I'd rather not wake up to disturb the experience.

Lea has been instrumental in assisting me with the interior decorating and the furnishing of "our" grand 5,500 square foot, country home. It may be more appropriate, however, to say that I have been assisting her.

With our July wedding date approaching faster than we will probably realize, I'm sure home improvement plans will take an eventual secondary role to plans for the wedding.

Although I've only known Lea's mother and a few of her close relatives for a short time, they seem to be a merry lot and are very kind to me. It's to be expected, I suppose, since one of their kin will soon be marrying a multi-millionaire. It's funny, but I still get goose bumps when I think about how wealthy I am.

"Will, we should go out and find another situation to solve and help someone in need."

"I think you may be right. A new year is upon us and our new journal is blank. What do you suggest? A trip to the mall may be in order. It seems like any time we are out in public you find someone who needs assistance in one way or another."

Oro appeared to think about the idea for a moment and then answered (telepathically, of course) with, *"Yes, the mall would be a good place to start."*

"OK. Let's get ready and we'll head that way."

"I'm already ready," offered a smiling Oro. *"I'm like baloney, I'm always ready."*

"Oro, you are just too funny today."

It wasn't long before we left Rainbow Acres in search of a new "client". The last mission Oro and I accomplished occurred right before Christmas and involved a brother and sister who were at the mall together. I reflected back on the occasion that began in Towne West's mall parking lot; our current destination.

I was out for some last minute gift shopping. Oro, as usual, was with me to keep me company. I found a spot on the outskirts of the huge lot and parked. A boy and girl, of preteen ages, walked passed the truck. I assumed them to be brother and sister. Oro had "heard" from the young girl and relayed her thoughts on to me. They involved finding "Santa" to ask him to bring her mom home for the holidays. That was the only thing on the girl's mind.

I left him in the truck and followed the kids through the mall's main entrance. Sure enough, they went straight for the "North Pole Depot", as it was called. It was an area, partitioned off by split-rail fencing, where "Santa" was available to hear kids' wishes. And to commemorate the event, parents could, for five bucks, get a picture of their child with him.

The girl I was concerned with had made her way to the head of the line, jumped into the not-so-jovial fat man's lap and promptly did ask him to bring her mother home for Christmas. "St. Nick" was a little taken back by the request, but asked the girl where her mother was.

"In jail," was her reply.

Now Santa's stand-in and I were both somewhat stunned by the answer. He told her that he dealt with gifts and toys and wasn't sure if he could help her. The adorable lass left with a depressed look on her face.

The brother, who had not appeared to be interested in the opportunity to sit on anyone's lap, had waited for his sister outside the scene of the North Pole workshop. I followed them down the long aisle towards the same door they had entered. Once outside, I came close enough to the pair to quietly ask if I could help them. When I had their attention, I added that I had heard of the girl's request.

"The Santa here," I said, "only deals with toys and such and that's why I was summoned. I handle special wishes from kids." OK, so I lied a little, but it was for a good cause.

I learned their names were Lacy and Lex and they relayed to me some eye-opening information about the situation. Their mother, Laura Lewis, was in the local lock-up for theft. After telling the two kids I would investigate the problem and get back with them, I departed. Oro was elated to hear the follow up story to his initial sensory interception.

"Great," he had thrown out, *"let's go to the slammer."*

Since I had stuck my nose into the affair, I saw no other choice but to go forward with what I had promised the youths. At the city jail, I told the desk sergeant that I was Laura Lewis' uncle. I know, another falsehood, but I felt it was necessary. After discussing the charges with him, I decided to provide the money for her bail. Processing her out, I was told, would take about half an hour. I asked permission to see her in the meantime. He said to take a seat and wait for her to be called up to the visitation area, where I would be allowed five minutes.

The few minutes I initially had to wait were about all my rear could take sitting on the uncomfortable, former church pew, turned public seating bench. My name was called and I was directed through a set of barred gates that closed behind me with a loud BANG! I had feelings of claustrophobia and beads of sweat began to form on my brow.

I walked down a desolate-looking hallway to a closed door. "Chat Room" was stenciled on the outside. I opened it and was met by an imposing man in uniform. I was shown to a little booth with a phone on each side of a panel of glass. It was like a scene from any one of hundreds of cop movies. I took a seat on a metal folding chair that was just as uncomfortable as the pew. A woman entered the adjoining room and was directed towards my location. She sat down opposite me with a bewildered expression. We picked up the available phones at the same time. I spoke first and told her I realized she didn't know me, but I was there to help get her home for Christmas to fulfill a wish by Lacy. The young woman began to cry.

"Bless you, Sir," was all she could manage to say.

I told her not to worry and she was able to offer a narrow smile before she left. I returned the same way I had come in and was relieved to find fresh air outside the bars, although it might have only been part of my imagination.

The sergeant told me she would be out soon. The official charge against the woman was for shoplifting at the mall, where Oro and I had seen her children earlier. After enduring a few more minutes of agony on the bench, I saw Laura coming down the passageway. A woman officer escorted her to a nearby counter where she picked up a paper sack filled with, I assumed, her personal items. As she approached me, a big smile now took the place of her previous distraught look. We left the jail and the air outside was positively much fresher.

Laura was pleasant looking enough and probably was even attractive in the right environment, but being in the "clink" had to take some of the glamour out of a person. I walked her to my truck to meet Oro and she began to tell me her tale of woe. She said she had no money to buy presents for Lacy

and Lex and had been caught stealing several things. Both
of her kids loved to read and the items she tried to take were
children's books from the mall's bookstore. I informed Laura
that removing her from jail was not all I was prepared to do
for her and she should not worry about the situation. This
news brought her to tears again.

We drove to her house where her mother was said to be
watching the kids, but I knew she hadn't been with them
earlier at the mall. After I pulled into the drive, the front
door burst open and the two children raced out. They ran
up to their mother and consumed her with big hugs. After
the initial excitement had subsided, Lacy eyed me and
exclaimed, "It's Santa's helper!"

Laura gave me a quizzical look. I told her I would call
later and explain. I slipped her four fifty's in a handshake
and wished the three of them a "Merry Christmas".

I informed Oro that we were going back to the mall where
Laura had been apprehended.

"What are you going to do there?" he had wondered.

I told him I was going to talk to those who had Laura
arrested. Once there, I went inside and visited with Emily
Youngers, the bookstore manager, about the situation and
after a lengthy and polite conversation, she agreed to drop
the charges.

That evening, I phoned Laura and told her the good news.
She was, of course, very pleased and appreciative of my help.
She told me she would find some way to repay me for the "loan",
as she put it.

The result of Oro's ability to read Lacy's mind had made
several individuals, including myself, very happy. "Oro," I
had said, "again, I get all of the credit for what you initiate."

He had smiled at me (he really does smile) and offered, *"We
are a team, Will, so it doesn't matter who gets the glory."*

At the present time, however, our hunt to find someone

to help proved futile. The thoughts Oro was able to make sense of did not require our "professional" assistance. A few examples were: A man was mad because he had left his shopping list at home, a woman was angry with how her hair looked after spending eighty bucks on it at the salon, an elderly couple was upset about the high cost of toys and there were numerous complaints about how "other" people drove and parked, etc.

"Oro, it's like the old saying, 'the best laid plans of mice and men often go awry'."

I have always loved throwing in old sayings, proverbs or famous quotes into my conversation with others and I made no exception in speaking with Oro.

"I suppose that goes for 'dogs and men' too, then?"

"I guess it does," I said, "but tomorrow is another day."

CHAPTER 2

LOST CHILD

I TURNED ON the TV to watch the noon news. The first topic presented was a full scale "Amber Alert" concerning a missing three-year-old child. Reports were sketchy, since the story had just broken, but it appeared that a young girl simply walked out of her house while the mother was taking a nap. A news crew was being dispatched to the scene to cover the story.

Lea called, while on her lunch break at school, to see if I had heard about the lost child.

"It would seem to me that a child of that age could not go far in this kind of weather," she said.

"I agree. It's just above freezing now and not expected to get much higher."

We chatted for awhile before she had to return to her class. I never gave much more thought to the matter until a newsbreak occurred about an hour later. The girl was still missing after an initial search of the immediate area. Volunteers were being requested to assist the police in their efforts to locate the child.

"Will," Oro quickly communicated to me, *"maybe we should go help."*

"That's a thought. I'm sure they would welcome us, but ..." I couldn't think of a good reason not to assist, so I amended my sentence. "Oh, why not? You've been looking for some action, since we struck out at the mall the other day. They'll probably find her before we get there, but it's worth a shot."

I bundled up to prepare for being out in the elements

and we left within minutes of making the decision to help. On the way to the area, I called and left a message on Lea's cell phone to let her know where we were going.

Parking near the scene had been wishful thinking, since the entire neighborhood, for blocks around, was inundated with vehicles. The response to help in the search was impressive, especially for a Friday afternoon. Oro and I made our way to a command center bus that was positioned in front of the missing child's home.

After signing in to help, we were put with a group of about twenty others with a patrolman in charge. He was given a grid of a particular area to search. We all marched, in a poor fashion, north of the center for four blocks to one side of a heavily wooded creek. Another group of people followed us and took up a position on the other side of the creek. Our leader told us to spread out in a line with about eight feet between each person. He informed us that the area had been walked before, but they had gone through it rapidly looking and calling out for a child they believed to be alive. Those in charge of the search effort now felt that the young girl probably would have succumbed to the affects of the cold. Therefore, our group was directed to thoroughly inspect the area for the girl's body.

There had been a lot of conversation and even laughter on our way to the creek, but virtually no one spoke after we were told what our task was to be. The only noise heard now was the rustle of the grass and breaking of sticks and brush underfoot. During the next hour and a half, we covered a swath through a one mile stretch of creek line and its adjoining field, with no positive results.

We were told to return to the command bus, if we chose to stay, for further assignments. By the time Oro and I reached our destination, half of our group had disappeared. They undoubtedly had returned to their vehicles and called it a day. We noticed a crowd of news people outside the command center and managed to worm our way to the front edge of the reporters, their photo crews and other citizens.

A young couple, escorted by a police captain, emerged from the bus and made their way right past our position to a stand of numerous microphones. The officer spoke to those present.

"Our failure to recover the child, even with all the available resources we've had on scene throughout the day, has led us to believe that the girl has been abducted by an unknown person or persons." He then introduced Ima and Ira Fink, the parents of the missing girl. The husband's brief talk to the crowd was a plea for the safe return of Marie, their daughter.

I won't go on to note what else was said at the briefing, because something even more newsworthy occurred. Oro requested my attention and "told" me to follow him, for he knew of a significant clue in the case. I couldn't imagine what could be so important, but I had never known him to lead me astray. After we cleared the throng of people, he elaborated.

"Will, the child did not walk out of the house and ..."

I interrupted him with, "Oro, the captain just told everyone that."

"You didn't let me finish. The child wasn't abducted either. The mother either gave, or even worse, sold the girl to someone."

"What?"

"I picked up from the mother something about how she hoped they didn't see the news and were smart enough to keep quiet about Marie."

"That is incredible. What a mess this has turned out to be. We must think this over and figure out what to do about what you know. Was there anything else?"

"Wasn't that enough?"

"Yes ... I suppose so. I must tell the police, but they might lock me up if I explain how I came across the information."

The press conference must have ended, for the assembly of people began to break up and depart in every direction.

A gentleman, walking along with a German shepherd, approached Oro and me with greetings. The dog wore a bright yellow vest with "SEARCH & RESCUE" stenciled on each side. We swapped names and struck up a conversation, while Oro and the canine stranger sniffed each other.

The man was about fifty, stood over six feet and I must say a good-looking fellow and not just because of his well trimmed beard and mustache like the one I sported. He also had what appeared to be a full head of hair under his cowboy hat. I miss not having an ample supply of growth under the ball caps I wear.

"I recon that's the end of the search," he said. "I'm sure the dogs enjoyed the exercise and the thrill of the hunt more than we did."

"Yes, I expect they did. So, Neal, are you with the police?"

"Not any more, Will. Max and I retired from the force last fall. What's Oro's specialty?"

"Well, he's not officially trained or certified, but he is special. He has insight in many areas that make him quite unique."

Neal paused and appeared to be considering what I had said before countering with, "Yes, dogs, I've found, have many abilities that humans aren't usually aware of."

"I'd have to concur with your observation. Say, Neal, do you happen to know the officer in charge?"

"Sure, Captain Rigley and I go way back. He was the lieutenant in charge of the K-9 Unit that Max and I were with, before he was promoted and reassigned last summer. His leaving was a major reason behind my decision to retire. In fact, he's the one who called me to come out and help."

"Do you think you could arrange a meeting with him for me about the present situation?"

"I don't see why not. Watch Max for me and I'll go check."

After Neal left, Oro and I "chatted."

"This dog is huge, Will," Oro offered with a sigh. *"He's pushing me around as if I were a puppy."*

"Well, I'm sure he outweighs you by at least thirty pounds."

"If you don't control him better, Will, I may soon need medical attention."

I pulled Max to one side and asked, "Say Oro, would you like to get into some kind of search and rescue training classes?"

"We seem to have a lot of time on our hands lately, so I'd be willing, if you want to check into it."

Neal soon returned with the captain and after the initial introduction, I decided to relate to him a round-about version of what Oro had learned. I was concerned that I might appear to be a wacko.

"Captain, I can't back up what I have to say with evidence, but I must report an educated suspicion that I have. The mother of the missing girl knows where her daughter is or at least who has her. I don't know if the father is involved or not, but the mother either gave or sold the girl to another couple."

The officer said nothing for a brief time. He must have been sorting out what I had just dumped on him. Neal also appeared to be somewhat perplexed over my statement. He kept looking back and forth between the captain and me, as if waiting for one of us to speak. Captain Rigley finally obliged.

"You say the girl was given away or sold to someone else. Do you know who has her?"

"No and what I told you is all I can tell you, because that is all I am aware of at this time."

"At this time," he repeated my words slowly and continued. "Do you mean to say that you may find out more?"

"Not necessarily," I nervously replied. I felt like I was getting in too deep. I began to think that revealing my unsubstantiated story may not have been a very good idea.

"Are you a psychic?" Neal asked.

I chuckled briefly and replied, "I don't profess to be one, but at times things come to me in ways I can't explain to you."

"I see," the captain retorted, but I was certain he really didn't.

"Let me ask you this, Captain," I added. "Is it possible for us to interview the parents?"

"Us?" he replied, in a form of a question.

"Yes, our little group here."

I could tell he was mulling the idea over in his head, for he failed to respond right away. I wanted Oro to let me know what was going on in the guy's grey matter."

He did with, *"Will, don't worry. He doesn't think you are crazy. He's just trying to figure out if it would be legal to let you interview the parents."*

I thought this was the perfect time to throw a little mystic into the fire.

"Captain, I'm not saying that I would conduct the interview. I would, of course, let you do that, but I do have one question I would like for you to ask them, but we'd have to be there to hear their response."

My comment, that answered his thoughts, must have spooked him some, from the expression that formed on his face, but he calmly replied with, "I suppose I could swing that, since I'm currently in charge of the whole mess. So what's the question?"

"OK, I'd like you to ask them if there is anything at all that they know about the girl's disappearance, which they aren't telling you. I would suggest you read them their rights before asking them the question."

"In my book," the captain responded, "they aren't suspects in the affair. I don't think giving them the Miranda bit is necessary."

"That's fine sir, it's only a recommendation."

"Neal, give me a few minutes and then bring Mr. Jacobs into the bus."

"Right, Cap."

In a short time, we headed towards the bus. Neal asked one of the officers to hold the dogs for us, but I told him I wanted to keep Oro with me. I don't know what I would have done if he had declined my request, but I didn't have to worry about it. He told the officer to disregard the request and we entered the command bus, with our dogs.

We joined the parents, the captain and a female officer around a long fold-out table. After we were seated, the woman officer pulled out a small tape recorder, turned it on, sat it in the middle of the table and began to read the couple their rights.

The captain had decided to go along with my suggestion. Neither parent requested an attorney. The husband said they had nothing to hide, but his wife was silent. The captain started the meeting by stating who was at the table and included the date and time of the "conversation" as he put it. Then a thought from Oro came to me.

"Will, the woman is very nervous and is wondering what we are doing here and what the police may have found out."

Captain Rigley then asked the Fink's a modified version of the question I had offered him. Within moments, Oro responded to me.

"She is afraid that Barb may have been intimidated by all the press coverage and turned herself in."

I scribbled a note on a pad of paper in front of me and gave it to Neal. He looked at it and passed it on to Rigley. I had jotted down the following: "Ask the mother if she knows a woman by the name of Barb."

He took the note, read it, folded it in half, put it in his pocket and paused for a moment. He then spoke to the husband. "Would you and your wife be willing to take a polygraph?" The question surprised me as it did the couple.

Ira responded with a twinge of anger. "Absolutely ... as I've said, we have nothing to hide." His wife still remained silent, but looked even more nervous.

The captain slowly slid forward in his chair, looked hard at the wife and said, "Mrs. Fink, do you know of a woman named Barb?"

The color in the woman's face went from white to pink. She slumped back in her chair and exclaimed, "That witch! I was worried that she wouldn't keep her blasted mouth shut and here it was all her idea in the first place." Her husband looked dumbfounded and seemed unable to speak.

Captain Rigley looked at me, then at Neal and said, "I believe you gentlemen can leave us now. I will, however, need a statement from both of you."

As we rose together, the woman gazed at me in anger with definite hate in her eyes and declared, "How did you find out?" I only shrugged and left with Neal and the dogs.

Once outside, Neal looked at me in amazement and followed up the woman's question with, "All right Will, how did you know about Barb?"

"Neal, it's rather complicated. Maybe one day we can get together over a cup of coffee and I'll tell you a little story."

"I'm going to hold you to that," he responded.

After writing a rather brief and hurried statement, Oro and I left. He cued me shortly after we began our trip home.

"What a story! Lea will never believe it."

"Oh, I'll bet she will. She knows what an extraordinary pair of sleuths we are."

We arrived at Rainbow Acres shortly after darkness had set in. Oro and I both received welcome home hugs from Lea, who said she had just returned from grocery shopping after school and was surprised that we were still gone.

"I received your message, but was beginning to worry about you, especially when I heard on the radio that the search had been called off. I thought I was going to have to go out and search for you boys."

"We are fine and we'll fill you in after we watch the news, for I'm sure a major development in the case is forthcoming."

It wasn't long before the six o'clock news aired with the lost child story as their lead. They showed a tape of segments from the first news conference of the day and then a more recent one where Captain Rigley calmly stated that an arrest had been made in the case with at least one other arrest expected. The "lost child's" mother was initially charged and jailed for making a false police report with other charges pending. He also spoke of a woman in Topeka who was being detained for questioning. The missing girl was found with that individual and was being returned to her father, who had not been charged in the case.

Evidently the Fink family had been in financial difficulty and the wife, who had not particularly enjoyed motherhood in the first place, had accepted money from an old school friend, in exchange for the child. The Topeka woman could not have children of her own and had been turned down in several attempts to legally adopt one.

After the segment concluded, Oro and I filled Lea in on our parts in the episode.

"That is absolutely unbelievable. How fortunate it was that you two decided to help in the search."

"Will, we should open up our own detective business. We could be called Crime Busters."

"Cute, Oro," I said and told Lea of his comment.

"Oro, that is cute. You and Will do make a great team."

From Lea's demeanor, it appeared that she was somewhat down in the dumps, for some reason. I asked Oro about her mood later and, sure enough, he had an answer for me.

"Lea feels that she is on the outside and not part of the 'team', as she put it."

"I see. We will have to make sure to include her more in what we do in the future."

CHAPTER 3

LEA ASKS FOR HELP

IT WAS FRIDAY again and a day of the week that I looked forward to, because Lea had reserved most of her weekends to spend time with Oro and me at Rainbow Acres. The newly acquired grandfather clock began to sound its low-base-pitched bongs. When they stopped after six, I saw the Wrangler coming up the drive to the house.

While on vacation last summer, it was evident how much Lea had loved the Jeep, so I let her have it. That was my plan from the start anyway, if our relationship evolved to a higher level. She had protested, at first, but only with a weak effort and there was no need for any major arm-twisting on my part. I told her she could sell her car and keep the proceeds, plus the Jeep, but she ended up giving the older vehicle to a niece, who was going away to college.

"Will!" Oro anxiously informed me. *"Lea's here. Let's go greet her."* We did and he was as excited about her arrival as I was.

"Hello Dear and Oro," she said with one of her beautiful smiles.

A period of hugs, kisses and pats on the head (for Oro) ensued, but not for long, since it was quite cold outside.

"Come in Doe, before we all freeze."

I began calling her "Doe" in Colorado after she started calling me "Dear" which she used not only as a term of endearment, but also to avoid many sentences with two "wills" in them. For example: "Will, will you help me?"

"We already have a nice cozy fire going inside to take the chill off."

"How nice Dear. It certainly has turned cold, but it is January, so it's to be expected."

The three of us settled down in front of the fireplace's immense hearth. Even though I purchased several cords of firewood specially ordered to be cut in two-foot lengths, the pieces still appeared to be small in the almost cave-like space. Our chimney was one that Santa would have no trouble coming down. The fireplace, however, did fit the room, due to its spaciousness. Lea and I had not found the time to come close to filling most of the rooms with furniture, for they were all large. We would get there one day and it had been fun shopping for antique furniture and new pieces that looked old.

The blaze of a fire inside or outside seems to act as a magnet to the eyes of those in its presence. This phenomenon held true on this crisp, late afternoon. The crackling of wood being consumed by the fire and the tick of the old grandfather clock were the only sounds to be heard until Lea spoke.

"Will, what would you say about the idea of having our wedding reception here instead of at a church? Rainbow Acres is such a lovely place and everyone in the family who attended the party last month can't wait to be invited back."

"It's an interesting idea, but it would take a lot of work and more planning."

"Just think about it Dear and we can discuss it later."

"Well, on a possibly related subject, do you remember Laura Lewis?"

"Yes, if you are speaking of the woman you bailed out of jail before Christmas."

"That's the one. I thought of her the other day while Oro and I were at the mall during our search for another Good Samaritan deed to perform. I called her to see how she and the kids were getting along. She has obtained a second waitress job and trying to make ends meet, but I guess the long hours are really getting her down."

"I can understand that," Lea interjected. "Being on ones feet at two jobs for hours has to be difficult."

"Well, after chatting back and forth with her about nothing important, a thought came to my mind."

"Oh no Will, what did you get yourself into this time? You and Oro have formed a great team to help others, but at times you have gone a little overboard."

"This is true Doe, however, when one makes the commitment to help another he should, in my opinion, follow the task through to the end."

"Will, when you helped break up the robbery at the convenience store last summer the end could have been the real end."

"Well, you have a point there, I agree, but everything turned out OK in that situation."

"All right then, tell me about this new idea of yours."

"Well, I asked Laura if she would be interested in starting a residential and commercial cleaning business. She informed me that she used to do that part time with a neighbor of hers, before Lex was born. I offered to set her up in the business if she was interested. She could start out doing the work herself to get established and then hire others to take on more clients. I know this place is going to require outside help to keep it up. I also know others who might be interested in hiring a regular cleaning service."

"So you don't feel that I can keep the house clean enough?"

The look on Lea's face was one I hadn't seen before. I believe I had, unintentionally, insulted her.

"No, no, no, it's not that. I just don't want you to be overburdened with the task. That would be too much to expect, especially with the time your teaching requires. In fact, Tana Taylor, from the real estate agency, told me that the previous owners had a live-in nanny who did the housework, cooked the meals and helped with the care of their young child. I feel you will need and deserve the help. Doe, the bottom line of the matter is that I would rather you spend more time with me than being behind a vacuum cleaner. Pretty selfish of me, huh?

"I see." She paused for a moment and then continued. "I do appreciate your thoughts, because it is a large home. I know you can afford anything, but I don't want to go out of my way to take advantage of the fact and spend money for you." She paused again. "All right, if the woman wants to take you up on your offer, it will be fine with me."

"Good. I told Laura to give it some thought and get back with me. She insisted that I come up with some ways for her to work off her debt to me for the "loan" at Christmas. I'm sure she would be interested in helping with the reception if we had it here."

"At least she is trying to be a responsible adult. I have never heard you mention the husband. I assume there is a story about him."

"Well, from what I gather, he split right after Lacy was born and has never been seen since, nor has he helped with the costs of raising the kids."

"Men can be such deadbeats."

"Yes Doe, I can't say I disagree with your comment in many cases. Not to intentionally change the subject, but how have your classes been going since the Christmas break?"

"Fairly well, but I am having some difficulty, over what is to be expected, with a few students. It always takes some time to become familiar with a new class of kids, but there are at least three that I have been unable to establish a good rapport with. Two of them are flunking and one is so close, she might as well be. The sad thing about the situation is that they seem to be good kids and are not a disciplinary problem to me."

"Yes, we've all had them, but sometimes you can't help them, because they don't want your help or anybody's help for that matter. You just have to move on and not take it as a personal defeat."

"Oh I know, Dear. It's not as if I have never flunked

anyone before, because I have. These students are not like some, who are belligerent, rude and even mean. They are decent kids. They are not troublemakers at all, but I can't seem to get them motivated. I have had conferences with the parents involved and they all claim there is nothing going on at home to indicate a reason for their poor efforts in school. I have also spoken with Counselor Woods, who has visited with each student and their respective parents."

"I'm sure you've been thorough and checked with their other teachers. How are they doing in those classes?"

"From what I gather in our team meetings, they are just getting by, but the other freshman teachers have not taken any extra time with them. Some teachers are not concerned as long as the kids are passing and that is just not right in my opinion."

"Well, in their defense, there aren't enough hours in the day to devote very much one-on-one time to individual students. The state and even the school system often expects too much of teachers. I will have to admit, I didn't always do as much as I should have because of time. Teachers, you know, are supposed to have a life of their own, just as much as anyone else."

"I understand the dilemma, Will, and I know when we are married our private life will, and should, take more of my time away from what I have been devoting to school."

"No disrespect to your students, but I'm glad to hear that." I then turned to Oro and said, "You do realize, big guy, that our time together will probably be curtailed some too?"

"That's understandable," he offered, *"and only right, but it's not like you're going to lock me up, are you?"*

"No, but there may be times when we shut the door on you, uh ... ya' know, for the sake of privacy."

"Oh, I get it," he conveyed to me and I could have sworn he was blushing. I may have been as well when I repeated the discussion to Lea, who then spoke directly to Oro.

"Oro, you are a most important part of the family and always will be. As a matter of fact, I wanted to discuss those students of mine who need help and Will unknowingly led the conversation directly to the subject. Are your talents and uniqueness rubbing off on him?"

"Possibly ... I have noticed he has had a heightened sense of awareness and insight lately."

"Well Oro," I said, "I've learned that I have to keep on my toes and be prepared for anything, because at times you manage to get us into some peculiar situations."

I repeated to Lea what Oro had expressed to her. To Lea I said, "So, did you want to know what I would do in your situation?"

"Actually, I was going to ask if Oro would help me with the problem. Oro, I really feel that if you could spend some time with the three, you could find out what problems they have that they are not sharing with anyone."

"I would be glad to help you Lea, if you think I can. What do you want me to do?"

"Lea, he's up for the challenge and if he can't help you, then no one can. He wants to know what you want him to do."

"Actually, nothing different from what he does when he is out with you. I have the principal's approval to meet with each student separately over my plan period during next week. He looked slightly confused when I informed him that I would be bringing a dog into the class with me, but he's open-minded and told me to do whatever I had to do."

"I've always known Mr. G. to be fair and responsive to teachers."

"Yes, he is. My talk with the kids will be casual and non-threatening, to allow them to open up and feel free to express themselves in any way. Oro will be there to observe and do his thing. That will give him about an hour to hopefully come up with something. What do you think, boys?"

Oro was the first to express his thoughts with, *"The length of time is ample enough, but what bothers them may be such that they don't want to think about, much less talk about."*

I told Lea of Oro's comment and then gave her my own thoughts on the subject.

"Oro might be right, but it's certainly worth the effort. After all, if Oro learns anything from the meetings, it was more than you had to go on before. When do you want to do this?"

"Monday morning works for me, if it's convenient with you. You could bring Oro to the front entry at ten or a few minutes after. That is when my planning time begins."

"OK, I can manage that. What about you, Oro? Are you free at ten on Monday?"

"Uh ... let's see ... Monday at ten. Mmmm ... yes, Lea, I'm available."

I tried to quote back to Lea not only what Oro had revealed, but also how he was "saying" it, but I was cracking up. I'm sure my secondhand version wasn't as funny.

"Oro, I wish there was a way for you to communicate with Lea, like you can with me."

"If I knew how to do that, I would certainly do it," he replied.

Later, I assisted Lea (OK, I watched and waited) in the preparation of a light meal of sandwiches and salad. Oro took up his normal position on a large padded mat in the kitchen to oversee the operations, as well. After the meal, we viewed a movie on the tube and retired for the night.

Lea hadn't always stayed overnight at Rainbow Acres. After lengthy and delicate negotiations, I was finally able to talk her into spending the weekends with us. She had rights to the master bedroom, with the fully modernized and enlarged bathroom. I vowed to continue to respect her privacy and to live by the same rules we had agreed upon, while we were on vacation together last summer.

I slept upstairs in one of the four original bedrooms. We decided to furnish only two of the rooms as actual guestrooms and keep our options open on what to do with the remaining two spaces. I had thought of a game room for one and no, we did not reserve the fourth one to be a nursery.

CHAPTER 4

ORO GOES TO SCHOOL

MONDAY MORNING ARRIVED on schedule, although Oro had wanted time to speed up, because he was more than ready to apply his skill to assist Lea. He had been "talking" about it most of the weekend and must have felt much like a racehorse in the starting chute, when the gate wouldn't open.

Lea had just left the house for school when the phone rang. Captain Rigley's name showed up on the caller ID's screen. I hadn't even had the opportunity to begin my second cup of coffee. I reluctantly answered the call.

"Captain, what a pleasant surprise."

"Jacobs, I've been thinking of the little session in the bus the other day."

He paused, so I chipped in, "I hope my statement was adequate, sir."

"Oh, I'd have to say it was too short, not very accurate, nor complete, but that's not what I'm calling you about."

"OK, what is it then?"

"I'm still a little puzzled as to exactly what happened in the bus. You say you aren't psychic, so can you explain to me, off the record of course if you choose, how you came up with the name, Barb?"

"No, I can't explain what happened ... the name just came to me, as I told you before."

This was not a lie, since it actually had come to me from Oro.

"Yes, that's what you said. Anyway, I'd like you to speak to, or at least listen to, an individual who I have in protective custody. I want to see if you can obtain some information from him."

"What do you want to find out?"

"Anything you learn may help us."

"I suppose I could give it a shot. Do you want me to come down to the station?"

"No, I'll pick you up in a minute."

"In a minute? Where are you?"

"I've just turned into your driveway."

"OK, we will be out shortly."

I hung up the phone and called to Oro. "Captain Rigley wants me to go with him to interview someone. You'll have to go too, since he wants to see if I can pull a cat out of a bag."

"What? Don't you mean a rabbit out of a hat?"

"There's no time to explain, but you'll figure it out," I said, as I rushed around to put on street shoes and grab a hat and coat.

"Will, just think about what is going on and I'll be able to understand."

"Oh, yeah, I always forget that I don't have to talk to you to get a message to you."

We met the captain outside on the porch. I told him we had an appointment at ten and he promised what he needed me for would not take long. He questioned my insistence that Oro come along, but he allowed him to accompany us.

Oro informed me, *"Rigley thinks you are weird, but he will overlook almost anything if you can really help him."*

The trip to a rundown warehouse on the west side of town took about twenty minutes. Talk between us had been sparse to non-existent during the trip. We entered a side door to the building and walked towards the middle of the large empty space to a card table with four chairs around it. A stocky man of about thirty occupied one of the seats.

A male and a female officer, both looking rather bored, stood on either side of the man. I recognized them from the command bus at the scene of the lost child episode. The lady cop again pulled out a tape recorder, like she had on the bus and placed it on the table. The other officer was the one I had given my statement to before leaving the area.

Captain Rigley offered me a chair and excused the two officers. We both sat down while Oro chose to stand (on all four feet) at my right side. Rigley spoke to the man we had joined.

"George, this is a friend of mine and ... uh, his dog. He is going to sit in on our conversation."

Oro's thoughts came through to me with, *"Will, there is something peculiar going on here. First off, the Captain thinks of the guy as 'Ben', not George and he's hoping he is as good an actor as he is a detective. Furthermore, Ben or George or whoever he is, is ticked off about giving up part of his day off for this little charade. I don't really understand what is going on."*

"I think I do," I said out loud.

"I beg your pardon," said Rigley.

"Captain, I think you can take us home now. I don't know what kind of game you are playing here, but it's wasting my time. This guy is not who you say he is. In fact, he's a police officer, isn't he?" I didn't wait for an answer. "Let's go Oro." I quickly rose and stormed for the exit.

Rigley caught up with me at the door and almost shouted, "Dat gummit, Will. If you aren't psychic then you explain to me what just happened here?"

"I don't have to explain anything to you," I said angrily. "You brought me here under false pretenses, so I think you should tell me what is going on."

"Jacobs," he began in a much calmer voice, "don't get into a tizzy. I'll fess up. I simply wanted to figure out a way to see if you were for real in your ability to know things that no one else seemed to know. I guess you proved yourself."

"Great, I'm happy for you. Now you can take us back."

"Hold your horses, man. I do need your help, but I had

to make sure that any information you happened to give me would be legitimate."

"OK, what do you really need?"

"I'm working on a tough case and I've tried everything I know to get to the truth, but have come up short."

"What kind of a case is it?"

"Murder! Are you interested?"

"Well." I swallowed some of my previous bitterness over the trick he pulled on us and added, "I guess you can count us in."

"Us? Are you saying that you have to bring the dog into this too?"

"Exactly. We are a team."

"Oh ... whatever. I need to work out a feasible plan on how I'm going to swing this and involve you in the right way. I'll get back with you."

"OK, give me a call, but you might think to give us more advanced notice next time."

With that, Rigley directed the woman officer to take us back. We were dropped off in time to leave for our trip to the school, where I met Lea at ten on the dot. She was all smiles, as she took Oro's lead from me.

"I'm really excited about what I have planned with Oro. I hope the time spent will be worthwhile. Can you meet us back here a little before noon?"

"Yes, Doe, in fact I'm just going to work on my column while parked here in the lot."

"Dear, you could come inside, if you'd like. I just thought you would prefer running an errand or something else."

"No thanks, I'll be OK out here."

"All right, then. I'll meet you back here at around twelve."

I returned to my Dodge Ram to work on my draft for this week's edition of "Grizzly's This 'N That," a humor column I had been doing for some time now.

The scope of the column had expanded, since several newspapers from around the state now carried it. I didn't make much money for the endeavor, but I enjoyed being creative. There was often no main direction to the piece. I would simply pull a subject out of the 'ole grey matter and expound on it for about five hundred words. The topics I often chose usually let me vent my frustrations of life in a harmless way, such as the dislike I have for waiting in lines, crying babies and people who lie to me for no particular reason. The acceptance of my column was also helping the sale of my first book, that bore the same title.

My topic this week dealt with how the word "guys" is used to refer to groups of people that include females. I've really been irritated over its use, ever since Lea and I dined at a nice restaurant (for a change) and the male server asked, "What can I get you guys?" If I'm not politically correct in calling him a waiter, it shouldn't be proper for him to include my fiancé in his lazy, generic use of "guys" in his speech.

I worked on the piece and had the rough draft finished by noon. As I approached the school's front entry, Lea and Oro exited.

"Hey, nice timing, Doe. How did things go?"

"I'm not sure, Dear, but I'm certain that something positive will come out of the meeting. You can take notes from Oro and let me know what he found out. We need to do the same thing for the other two kids over the next two days, if that's all right with you and Oro?"

I spoke for the two of us with, "We don't have any pressing issues on our calendar, so I see no problem at all."

"Great, I would really like to come over each evening to hear what Oro may have learned, but I have meetings after school tonight and tomorrow night. I will come by Wednesday evening to listen to Oro's report and in appreciation of your help, I would be happy to fix you both a nice home cooked meal."

"That's a deal that I'll hold you to, but I think I'm getting the best of the arrangement."

Before we left, I told Lea of our morning incident with Captain Rigley.

"That is somewhat bazaar," she remarked. "So you

passed his test, but he didn't tell you any facts about his murder case?"

"Correct. I expect we'll hear from him soon, but I won't cancel out on your project with Oro."

"Thank you, Dear and keep me informed on what happens with that story."

Oro and I repeated the procedure we had followed on Monday for the next two days. I would take him to school at ten in the morning and we were out of there by noon. Oro would tell me what transpired after each of the meetings. I would take notes on what he learned from the students.

Lea arrived shortly before five-thirty on Wednesday with some groceries. "Let's see what you have come up with, Oro," she said, "and then I will prepare dinner."

The largest room at Rainbow Acres would be called the living room by most folks, but we (mostly Lea) decided to call it the gathering place. It was probably Lea's favorite section of the house, especially when I took the time to build a fire in its huge fireplace. For the presentation of Oro's findings, I did choose to light a fire, but opted to use the much smaller and more convenient fireplace in the library/study. We (mostly I) couldn't decide on what to call my favorite room in the house, which was formerly the parlor room.

"Doe, we (mostly I) started a fire in the library as the place to discuss Oro's report."

"Lea, he may have 'started' the fire, since I'm not allowed to use matches, but I carried the firewood from the gathering place."

"I stand corrected," I said, and I informed Lea of Oro's assistance, as we proceeded to the library.

"Oh, how nice. The peaceful ambiance created by a nice fire in the fireplace is nearly magical. Will, will you ...

there I go again. Dear, why don't you read what you have, while I sit back, relax and digest the information."

"OK. You met with Jason on Monday. His problems appear to stem from a severe case of low self-esteem. He feels that no one likes him. He has no close friends. Other students, especially those above the freshman class, make fun of him for the way he dresses and looks. He knows he is skinny, but doesn't know what to do about it. He seems to be so upset, mentally, that Oro's afraid he may have considered suicide, especially after one of the boy's thoughts was 'nobody would care if I were gone from this world.'"

"Oh my!" Lea exclaimed. "That's not good, at all. I knew he was shy and reserved, but I would not have thought he was as depressed as that. His clothes are a mess, but I'm not saying they are dirty. They are always wrinkled, out of style and don't particularly fit well."

I could tell Lea was deep in thought about the boy, so I paused until she told me to continue.

"OK, next on the list comes Gina. Her parents, as you surely know, are divorced. She's not concerned about failing, simply because she wants to make her mother look like she isn't doing her job as a parent. In this way, Gina feels that her father will decide to request custody of her. It surprised me when Oro made it clear that she did not want to stay with her mom after the parents divorced. I personally don't know of any kids in families of divorce, who have gone with the father."

"Those divorce cases always affect the children more than parents realize. I knew there had to be something hidden in her case, because the girl is smart enough to do well. I even spoke with a couple of her eighth grade teachers, who said she did fine in school last year and the divorce occurred over last summer. This information, Oro, is very interesting and should help me. I have only spoken to Gina's mother and had no indication that the father might want custody, but he was never really discussed in our talk, so I will have to arrange a meeting with him. All right, what about Leslie?"

"Leslie, Oro feels, is just plain lazy. She doesn't care what her grades are. Neither of her parents requires her to do anything if she doesn't want to. They probably aren't authoritative at all and Leslie runs the show. She must be pretty much spoiled and she thinks school is boring and a waste of her time. She would rather just watch TV, listen to music or talk to her friends on the phone."

"That depiction of Leslie does not differ from anything that I have come up with about her or, for that matter, her parents. I could tell from my conference with them that they were not going to be supportive of my request. I wanted them to insist that Leslie do her work or lose TV and phone rights. I can see this will be a test of patience and intellect to make her come around. Oro, you were splendid. Thank you so much. If the secret ever gets out about you, all the teachers in our whole school district will want your help."

Oro's eyes seemed to beam with delight as he replied to her, *"I am glad that I could be of assistance. I enjoyed myself a lot too, so I should thank you. If you need me to be with any of the children again, just let us know."*

I again took the role of intermediary and repeated Oro's comment to Lea.

"So, now that you have some inside tips, what are you going to do?" I asked.

"I'm going to fulfill my obligation to you both and fix dinner," Lea replied.

"That will work for us, Doe"

Oro and I kept Lea company, while she prepared supper (or dinner or whatever you want to call it). We had a pleasant meal and she departed shortly before the ten p.m. news, after I helped her grade a stack of tests she had brought with her from school. The task gave me flashbacks of how boring the process of grading papers at home was, when it should have been personal time. Those who believe that teachers are paid well enough for the work they do, both in and out of the classroom, should try it themselves.

CHAPTER 5

ACCIDENT OR MURDER?

I WAS AWAKE, but still in bed, when the phone began to ring. I decided to let it do its thing for the prescribed amount of time before the answering machine would come to life. It was Captain Rigley and he was yelling. "Jacobs, pick up the darned phone".

I didn't, but it did me no good, for it began to ring again. I could see there was no use in putting off a "delightful" chat with the man, so I picked up the extension.

He began talking before I had a chance to acknowledge the call. "Hey sleepyhead, get your butt out of bed. A new day is dawning."

"Rigley, it's barely six. I haven't even made coffee yet. Call me back."

"Good morning to you too," he bellowed. "I thought you country people got up early in the day to catch worms or something like that."

"It's still dark, so to me it's still night. Besides, I only live in the country. I'm not a farmer who has to be up with his roosters."

"Whatever," he said. "I've figured out a plan of how you can help me with my situation. Put the coffee on."

"Don't even tell me you are pulling into my driveway, as we speak."

"Say, that's good. I should have done that. No, I'm at headquarters, but I'll be over before too long."

The line went silent. Oro was looking at me from the end of the bed through sleepy eyes. He commented on what had occurred.

"That guy is certainly rude, isn't he? He never even got your permission to visit."

"You could hear him?"

"Of course I could hear him. He's one of those loud talkers, who speak to everyone as if they are hard of hearing."

"Exactly. I suppose I should get some coffee made and prepare for our favorite public servant's arrival."

Rigley arrived on the short side of fifteen minutes, which surprised me. I opened the door. He strolled in, went straight to the kitchen and sat down. Under his arm was a large manila envelope.

"Nice place you have here. Pour me a cup, will ya. It really smells good. Black will do."

"You got here awfully fast for coming all the way from downtown."

"Red lights and siren – I never leave home without them," he said with a smile.

Actually, I had to hold back a smile myself. "OK, Captain," I said, while serving him up a cup of the freshly brewed French vanilla flavored coffee. "What's so important that it couldn't wait until daylight?"

"Oh, it could have waited, but why dilly dally around?"

"Thanks for your concern and let's cut to the chase, if you please."

"Jacobs, you're not too cheery in the morning are you?"

I didn't answer.

"At any rate, I have, as I said before, come up with a way that you can help me."

"OK, but I don't even know what you need help with."

"Impatient cuss, aren't you?"

"Actually, I'm not very patient, so please continue."

"Here's some background info. The recent ice storm the city experienced raised havoc everywhere and the demise of an elderly rural resident was being blamed on the weather."

"Yes, I heard on the news a story about an old guy who

was trying to clean up his yard and must have had a heart attack, but what's that got to do with murder?"

"Jacobs, I didn't agree with the coroner's initial explanation on the cause of death that the man simply slipped on the ice, couldn't get up and eventually froze to death."

"Well, you have my full attention, so go on."

"I believe that the man was murdered by his son, who used the frigid, near zero, temperature outside to aid in the deed."

"Why do you suspect foul play?"

"I'll show you why."

Rigley pulled numerous 8x10 photos from the envelope he had brought with him, placed them on the table and slid them across towards me. I picked them up and glanced through them with interest and then went through them for a second time.

"Well, Captain, I don't particularly see anything significant except for the presence of the walker. Could the man walk without it?"

"Good thinking Jacobs. The son, Mike Morgan, said he could, but I've been told by the daughter, Sharon, that he could hardly walk at all. She said that the walker was used several months ago, when he was still partially mobile. What are your thoughts or gut feelings?"

"Well for one thing, if the guy had to use the walker, how was he going to accomplish gathering up limbs in the yard?"

"Good point ... anything else?"

"Another concern I have is with the position of the walker. The photo seems to indicate that the man's direction of travel was to the right, but the prone body is in front of the walker and faces the left. He's not behind it."

"Hey, you should sign up to be on my team. I could use some people with natural insight instead of a criminologist degree with good grades. What else do you see?"

"Uh ... nothing, I guess."

"I'll tell you something that didn't look right to me.

Do you see how the body does not exactly fit the ground where he was found? Wouldn't it be logical to think that he would have been molded, so to speak, with the contour of the ground? I am sure that he died somewhere else and was placed in the yard."

"That is an interesting idea," I said as I glanced at the pictures, which supported his statement. "Who found him?"

"The area's rural postal delivery woman noticed him around noon the day after the storm. It had gotten so cold that everything was frozen solid, so there were no footprints to find. The autopsy conducted two days later pretty much confirmed what I believed. Blood pooling in the body indicated that the man died partially on his side and not exactly how he was found by us. The mail lady swears that she did not touch the body."

"Why do you suspect the son?"

"The old man's daughter indicated that he was hard up for cash and was in line to inherit a decent amount of money and a share of the property, if the long-retired farmer kicked the bucket. She indicated that Morgan senior had recently been to the doctor for a physical and the prognosis was good that he would be around for quite some time. The physician confirmed her story. I don't think the son wanted to wait for the inheritance. Money and the greed factor, in one way or another, seem to often play a major role in many crimes against others."

"I would imagine that would be true. OK, how do you feel I can help you in all this?"

"The plan is simple enough. I will have the surviving son brought down to the station for questioning. You will be in the room as a consultant in the case."

"Captain, you are forgetting about Oro. He should be in the room as well."

"What in the blazes is it with you and your dog?"

"To partially coin a phrase that you used earlier; I don't leave home without him."

"That's evident, but why does he have to be with us in the interview?"

"Let's just say that he gives me inspiration."

"How am I going to explain your dog's presence?"

"That's not my problem, it's yours, but where I go, Oro goes."

"Good grief. Let me think about it and I'll call you back."

With that he abruptly left, shaking his head all the way to the door. He left so fast that I didn't even see him out.

"Oro, I need some more coffee."

Before I had a chance to finish pouring me a fresh cup, the phone rang. It was, as expected, the captain.

"Jacobs, I've given it some thought. You can bring the … uh, mutt to the station with you."

"The words you must have been searching for is 'the dog' or you may call him by his proper name, 'Oro.'"

"Whatever. I've figured out a plan of attack, which may work out even better than my original idea."

"OK, when do you want us there?"

"One o'clock."

I was about to acknowledge the time, but the line went dead.

"He hung up on me again."

"Will," offered Oro, *"he must always be in a hurry and doesn't have the time to conclude conversations."*

"Well, at any rate, Rigley wants us to meet with him at one. I'm sure he thinks I'm screwy, since I insisted that you be with me again."

"Great, I'll be able to do some more undercover work."

After our arrival at the precinct, we were escorted to Rigley's office, by the "tape recorder lady." It was a surprisingly decent looking space. The oak furnishings were old, but from a time when quality meant something. His large desk was cluttered (I should talk) with stacks of files, but they were in a somewhat orderly fashion.

I would never have given furniture a second thought in the past, but I have become more observant and knowledgeable in the field. Furnishing the over 5,000 square foot home at Rainbow Acres has been a time consuming and not always enjoyable chore, but it was and continues to be an educational experience.

The majority of one wall in the office was delegated as Rigley's pictorial history in the department. It held a plethora of framed photos, in an array of assorted sizes, showing him with others. There were pictures of him rubbing elbows with local TV and radio celebrities, well-known city business leaders and a range of political figures, including state governors and Wichita's mayors of past and present. I even viewed him with no less than three former U. S. Presidents.

On another wall hung the captain's collection of medals, honors and awards he had received over the years. I learned from one framed certificate of service that his years on the force totaled over thirty. I was interrupted during my look back in time, when the door opened. It was Rigley and he was looking pleased (for a change) about something.

"Captain, I took the liberty to browse a bit. I'm impressed. What was it like to meet the Presidents of our nation?"

"Oh that. It was just in the line of duty, since I was in charge of security, along with the feds, of course, when they were in town for one thing or another. They were only photo ops and I never talked with any of them. My wife has tried to motivate me to explore the possibility of landing a White House job or an appointment somewhere, but I'm not personable enough to kiss up to anyone."

I made no comment as to his personality as I saw it. Evidently, he was already aware of his brusque manner. He was about my age, a little shorter and outweighed me by about twenty pounds, but he looked solid. He was certainly an imposing figure and probably "all work and no play" would have been his favorite motto. I could tell those around him respected him highly, but were probably afraid of him. He could be intimidating and I was pleased that I had stood my ground with him on earlier occasions. He seemed to appreciate, in the end, my frankness with him.

"Well sir, we are ready to go if you still require our assistance."

"Yeah, right! Here, put this on your dog."

He handed me a yellow K-9 Search and Rescue vest like Neal's dog Max had worn on the day of the search for the missing girl.

"You will be introduced as the handler of, uh, Oro, isn't it?"

"That's correct."

"Tell him that I appreciate him not calling me 'mutt,'" added Oro.

"OK."

"OK, what?" inquired Rigley.

"Oh, mmm, OK … I'm his handler; then what?"

"You probably won't have to say anything. My hope is that the guy will confess with the surprise questioning that I have planned for him, but if he doesn't, maybe you will come up with a clue in the case."

"OK, and thanks, by the way, for calling Oro by his name and not 'mutt.' He wanted me to tell you that."

Rigley only looked at me with a frown as I fastened the vest around Oro. We proceeded to follow him along the hallway outside his office, where we turned down a narrow corridor to the right and arrived at our destination after passing three, unmarked doors within a distance of about fifty feet. We entered a room, which was not nearly as pleasant as the one we left. It was like another cop scene taken from television or the movies. We had come to one of the interrogation rooms. The area was drab and a cold chill went up my spine as I took a seat at a small round table, which was centered in the space. The room was void of anything except the table with four chairs. On the wall opposite the entry was the always-present mirror, which everyone knew was of the two-way variety. I wondered who, if anyone, would be on the other side watching and listening to what was about to take place in the room.

A man was brought in by Officer Margaret (I grew tired of only knowing her as "the woman with the tape recorder", so I had found out her name). She directed the guy to take a seat across from Rigley. The captain reminded the man of his rights under the law. The popular tape recorder was again produced and turned on. The captain followed his procedure of stating the "who, what, when and where" spiel. Mike Morgan was of medium height and looked out of shape, due to his pot belly. His unshaved face was marked from skin problem scars and his deep-set, dark eyes made him look almost scary.

Rigley made mention of who Oro and I were and continued with various questions, which must have been asked before due to the man's irritation that was reflected in his speech and demeanor. Then the captain came out with the "surprise questioning" he had hinted about earlier.

"Morgan, Oro is one of two dogs that we used at the scene of your deceased father's home. They are the best tracking canines in the area. Max, the other dog, was offered clothing taken from your father's body to track his scent. The result of his search was quite peculiar."

He paused and took a sip from the coffee cup he had brought with him. The short delay may have been to see what reaction the man might have or to think about what he was to say next, since he was obviously making up the story.

Oro's thoughts came to me with, *"The man is very nervous and isn't quite sure what is coming, but he doesn't like it."*

The captain continued. "Mr. Morgan, the dog picked up no trail from any exit of the house and only keyed on the spot where your father was found. That fact, to me, was very odd, but the dog's handler told me what it meant. It meant that your father did not walk to where he was found, but that's not all." He again paused to drink from the cup.

Oro entered the mix again with, *"Will, Morgan can't believe that they thought to bring in dogs when the death surely would be seen as an accident. His last thought was that he wondered if they could possibly have found the spot where he put his father in the field behind the barn."*

I decided that the information Oro had given me warranted an interruption into the proceedings.

"Captain, may I have a word with you?"

Rigley didn't seem to be upset with my request. In fact, he appeared to be pleased by my intrusion.

"Certainly, Will."

We both rose and left the room.

"What is it?"

"Oro ... um ... uh, I believe Morgan must have carried his father to a spot in the field behind the barn. Does that make sense?"

"It does and it's what I suspected, because I was told that the man could not have made it, on his own, from the house to the yard where he laid, even with the aid of the walker, because he couldn't go down steps. You were about to say something about your dog. What is it? Does he need to go outside or something?"

"Oh, no, we are good to continue."

We reentered the room and Oro quickly notified me that Morgan felt his sister was somehow behind this and it was too bad that his efforts to get her out of the way earlier hadn't worked.

"Amazing," I thought, but I couldn't very well explain the new development at this time to Rigley, who had now continued with his questioning.

"Do you know what was also peculiar?" He didn't wait for an answer. "Oro, here, was set out to track your scent at the scene. He tracked you from the house to an area in the field behind the barn and also to the exact location where your father was found, but that's still not all. Max was allowed to roam the area and drew a hit of your father's scent in the field, west of the barn, at the same place where your trail had led Oro. But again Max found no trail to or from the field that was made by your father."

Rigley again paused to finish his cup of coffee, but continued to stare at the man. Morgan's posture was one of resignation. He fidgeted somewhat in his chair and wiped his forehead where sweat had formed. His face was red and he looked defeated.

"Mike," Rigley said in a more soothing tone, "why don't you tell us what happened."

After a long pause, Mike responded. "I carried Dad outside and put him in the pasture behind the barn and left. I came back after dark and moved him to the place beside the house."

It seemed like all of us in the room, except Oro, took a deep breath at the same time. The captain broke the silence.

"Why did you take him behind the barn?"

"I didn't want him to be seen from the road."

"Then why not take him behind the house?"

"There weren't any tree limbs down from the storm there and I wanted it to look like he was trying to clean up some of the mess."

"I see. Mr. Morgan, I will have to officially arrest you for the murder of your father."

"It wasn't murder ... he asked me to do it."

"What?" Rigley said with a slight choke in his voice.

"My dad didn't want to live anymore and wanted me to put him out of his misery."

"I suppose that will have to be decided by a jury," Rigley said. "Let's go."

Oro cued me with, *"Morgan is not telling the truth, Will."*

The captain told Margaret to take down Morgan's statement and have him sign it. We returned to his office where I didn't beat around the bush and spoke first.

"Captain, the guy is lying about following his father's wish and I did acquire another bit of info that may be interesting to you. He felt that his sister had something to do with your suspicion of him and wished that his efforts to get rid of her had not failed."

"That is interesting and I will check with the woman to see what that may be about. In the meantime, we did good work today, don't you think, Jacobs?"

"Yes sir, another case solved."

"I'd have to admit that I was going a little out on a limb in there. If I made an error in any way with the fake dog story, he would have figured out that I was bluffing. Your hint came in at the perfect time." He paused. "It was 'your' hint, wasn't it?" he said with a confusing, half-smile look on his face. "It's odd how things just happen to 'come to you', as you say. Don't you think?"

I didn't answer and was a little uncomfortable about my near foul up, when I almost revealed to the captain that Oro had given me the information. I believe Rigley, in the back of his mind, thought there was more to my association with Oro, than I was telling him.

I had gotten too used to quickly relaying my exchanges with Oro to Lea. I would have to be careful in the future around Rigley, for I knew he was an intelligent man.

I called Lea just before the early evening news aired and told her to pay attention to the story about the man who was found frozen in his yard a week earlier. She tried to obtain more information about the situation, but I told her to call me after she watched the segment.

She phoned me back within a few minutes.

"Will you must have had a reason for me to see the piece on the news. Are you telling me that you and Oro had something to do with that case, too?"

"We certainly did." It was now time to fill her in on our part of the investigation. I could tell by her occasional response of "Really!" that she was impressed with our parts in the whole story not presented in the piece on the tube.

Lea told me to congratulate Oro for her. "You two have hit the big time now, haven't you? Are you going to be tagging around with this Captain Rigley from here on out?"

"I don't think so, Doe, but I'm sure we will be at the top of his call list if he runs into snags with any of his cases in the future."

CHAPTER 6

MAKING THE GRADE

T HE MOOD AROUND the house had been rather subdued, especially for a Friday. Earlier in the week Lea had informed us that she was not coming to stay over after school today. Most of the women in her family were going out for the evening on a bachelorette party for Lea's niece, the gal who had received Lea's car, after I had given her the Jeep. Thankfully, Lea promised she would be over early the following morning.

I hadn't slept well overnight and didn't roll out of bed until much later than usual. Oro informed me that he had already been out for his morning ritual while I began mine with making coffee.

"Oro, what did you do with the paper?

"Oops, I forgot to get it. Hold on and I'll be back shortly."

Lea phoned just as he left the house and called to say she was on her way. I heard the large flap on the dog door slap shut as we concluded our call.

"I heard the phone ring while I was out. Was it Lea? Do you know when she is coming over?"

"One question at a time, please. Things are looking up now. My coffee's done perking and Lea said she was on her way and in the company of a pan of her homemade cinnamon rolls."

"That woman is too nice, Will."

"Yes, I agree. We are two lucky hombres."

Within a few minutes, Oro alerted me with, *"I believe I hear the Jeep pulling in,"* as he bounded towards the door.

It had arrived, but I hadn't heard it. The Jeep ran so smoothly that I could barely hear it running when I was outside, much less from inside the house, but Oro had no trouble hearing it from within and several hundred feet away. We greeted her in the drive and I quickly latched onto the pan of sweet-smelling rolls and started to make a dash to the house, but stopped short. I decided it only proper to escort Lea inside, while Oro happily trailed along between us.

"Boys," she said, "I am going to make you breakfast too, unless you have already eaten."

"You know me Doe. I'm not inclined to do anything for food in the morning, so fix away and I'll even force myself to save the rolls for dessert."

I always loved beginning the day with a hearty breakfast, but I've always been too lazy to fix the meal for myself. Fortunately for me, Lea was a firm believer in the notion that a good breakfast is the most important meal of the day.

Within a short time, we sat down to scrambled eggs, lean bacon strips, hash browns and pancakes; followed by the rolls. I thought I was at IHOP. After the meal, Oro and I helped with the cleanup duties. Oro licked the plates clean and I put them in the dishwasher. Whew! I was worn out and needed a rest. We all remained around the much used breakfast nook and exchanged idle talk. The area was added to the kitchen during the recent, large-scale remodeling project done on the place.

If Lea and I were ever bored, we could always go out in search of more furnishings for the home. Each room had a theme (per Lea's request). The kitchen faced the east and welcomed the sunrise with a springtime motif. Flowers of all colors dominated the space and always kept the area bright and cheery.

Several months had passed since Oro had assisted Lea in meeting with three of her students, so the conversation shifted to how things were going at school.

"Lea, do you have any progress to report on your wayward charges?"

"Let me answer your question with a question. Do you like baseball?"

"Oh … it's OK, but I generally only watch it during the playoffs or the World Series."

"I will use an analogy to baseball to describe how things are with the three. I hit a home run, a double, and made it to first base on an error, so overall I am pleased with the outcome."

"Well, two for three is great, Doe! I must say I'm impressed with how you began your presentation, but now be more specific."

"Leslie's situation is better in some regards, but other problems have arisen. Her previous apathy in the classroom has changed to that of being somewhat rebellious, because of my interference. I can tell that she resents my efforts to help, especially when I involved her parents in the process."

"They agreed, after meeting with the principal, the counselor and me, to obtain family counseling sessions to work on a plan to change the girl's indifferent behavior towards her studies in school. Since the sessions are private, of course, I am not aware of what plans they are developing within the family. Leslie has been required to carry a Student Evaluation Form. Her attitude rating and class assignments are listed on the daily form, which she has to take home and show to a parent for a signature. If she fails to return the signed sheet to the office, she is sent to the detention room, which is worse than being in any regular classroom."

"Leslie has been doing more than she ever did before, but the quality of her work is still below what I know she is capable of. I think she is only going through the motions, but I have not given up on her. I honestly feel that she will try to skate by during this school year. A positive change now and in the near future can only come about if her parents change their own lackluster approach to childrearing. They are, in many ways, mostly responsible for why Leslie's desire to learn and participate in school has declined. At least I did not strike out in her case, but it's still too close to call."

"If the parents don't follow through, it's not your fault, Doe."

"I know. At least Gina's situation is brighter now and I'm optimistic about her improvement in class. I had a private meeting with her father, who says he knew nothing of her problems in school. He was upset with his ex-wife for not keeping him informed. I had to be tactful about the information Oro found out from Gina. He told me of his intentions to meet with Gina and her mom to fully discuss the matter."

"He called me the next evening to let me know that the meeting had occurred and asked me to keep him abreast of his daughter's work. He said he had agreed to spend more time with his daughter and she was directed to work harder in school. Her attitude has changed somewhat and she has taken more of an active interest in her studies. If she keeps it up she will have no problem passing this year, but she still is not always a happy camper in the classroom."

"Well Doe, divorce, as you've said, is always hardest on the kids. They are caught up in the middle with usually no say in the affair (no pun intended), but someone said, 'time heals all wounds.' Check up on Gina next year and I'd bet you find a different young girl from how she is today."

"I hope you are right, Dear. Someone also said, 'I have saved the best 'til last.' I feel that I have made great strides in Jason's case, since he has advanced the farthest. I met with the school's counselor, nurse and nutritionist about Jason's health in body and in mind. The parents were informed of our concerns and scheduled Jason for a thorough physical exam. Parent interviews were conducted and tests were done as part of the evaluation. It was determined that the boy's diet was severely inadequate."

"In the meantime, I visited with the owner of The Fitness Center, not far from the school."

"Aren't they the ones who offered all teachers in the district half-priced memberships?"

"Yes, in fact, I am a member."

"I never considered joining it myself."

"It's not too late," Lea said with a grin.

"Uh ... yeah, right. Anyway, what happened next?"

"All right Dear, back to the subject at hand. Richard, the owner, contributed a one year membership to Jason and even signed him up with one of his personal staff trainers at no cost. A weight training program began two months ago and is showing good results."

"Our nutritionist at the school put Jason on a high carb and protein diet for a time, along with vitamin and mineral supplements. You have not seen the boy, but he is about my height, but weighed twenty pounds less. With the diet and training program, he has gained over ten pounds already and his energy level in the classroom has increased."

"On top of all that, your generous donation to the family to acquire new clothes for Jason has certainly made a big difference in his attitude and how he feels about himself. I can tell he is proud of how he looks now and his other teachers have told me the same thing. They want you to "adopt" some of their students for your next improvement project."

"Well Doe, I'm glad I could assist in your efforts to help the boy. Clothes may not make a person, but if one looks good it seems to help them feel good. It sounds like you have done a swell job and I'm sure you won't get all the credit that is due you for your hard work, which was certainly beyond what is expected of you."

"Jason has been doing much better in the grade department as well. I told him and the two girls that I would wipe the slate clean for this grading period if they would apply themselves and work to improve, but Jason has made the best turnaround. Everything he has turned in since Oro became involved has been "A" work. I thank both of you for what you have done."

Oro had been patiently sitting with us through Lea's commentary of her project to help the three students. He was now "heard" from.

"I am very happy that there has been positive improvement by the three. I expected that you would have success, but you exceeded even what I thought would be possible in the short term. I knew it would take time with the two girls to come around, but I was the most worried about Jason's frame of mind. I'd say you did a remarkable job on him, Lea."

I told Lea of Oro's comments and she sat on the floor and hugged him and said, "I could not have succeeded without your help Oro. While on the subject of help, do you two have any new 'clients', as you call them, that you are helping?"

"Not right now. Our slate is pretty much clear. I told you before about Laura accepting my help to set her up in a cleaning service. She has obtained the applicable licenses required, set up charges at two wholesale janitor supply companies and opened a business checking account at our bank, with my friend Luke, as her advisor. I co-signed a small business loan through him for her to purchase equipment and supplies. She isn't working at the restaurants any longer and is set to go. She has named her new enterprise "The Clean Queens", which I thought was fairly catchy."

"Yes, that is cute. So, does she have any customers yet?"

"Well, yes she does. As you know, I will be her first, but Luke, my financial advisor at the bank, has managed a nice deal for her. She will be in charge of cleaning the main bank and their three branch facilities beginning next month, when the contract with another cleaning service expires. I helped her put together a bid proposal that she presented to the bank. The bid was moderately lower than the business currently doing the work. They had the option to match Laura's quote, but declined. With the amount of work already lined up, I think she'll do fine.

"Will, is she going to try to do all the work by herself?"

"No, she actually has hired two other ladies, who were waitresses with her."

"I hope things work out for her. When will she begin cleaning here?"

"I'm glad you brought that up because she is coming by this afternoon. I told her she could bring her kids over to keep Oro occupied or maybe the other way around might be more accurate."

"You mean I get to have company?" inquired Oro.

"I hope that's OK with you and Oro."

"Certainly! We can play fetch."

"I asked Laura if she could drop by here for the afternoon, because I wanted some areas done now."

"Will, I feel that I should be here when she comes to clean. I don't know, maybe it's being territorial or some other Freudian thing, but I feel that I should be around."

"Doe, you are more than welcome to be here at any time."

"If it weren't for what people might say, I would permanently move over in the blink of an eye."

"Lea, I've suggested it more than once before. Why would anyone care? I would continue to honor your privacy as I have always done in the past, as if that's anyone's business."

She paused for a time before continuing. "All right, but you must twist my arm, but just a little, please."

"Outstanding!" I said as I reached across the table, held her wrist and followed the request with a gentle turn.

Oro, who was always present, came up with other jubilant words and, *"That is the best news we've had for some time."*

"Lea, let's go get some boxes and I'll help you pack."

She smiled and looked a little embarrassed.

"Actually, I have quite a few boxes already packed and ready."

"Well, you little fox, you. What are we waiting for then?"

We had time to make one trip for things at Lea's place before Laura arrived. It was going to be wonderful having Lea stay with us full time now and not have to wait for the July wedding. I had grown to dread Sunday evenings when she would return to her apartment for the week.

Oro, The "Tail" Continues

Now she would be here for good and Oro and I were elated. Lea confessed that she planned to agree to move in on a full-time basis the next time the subject was brought up. We would be a threesome again, just as it was six months ago when we acquired Oro at the campground near Durango.

CHAPTER 7

WILL BECOMES A "DAD"

L AURA ARRIVED RIGHT after the lunch hour, as she said she would. Lea had not taken time to eat, for she wanted to, as she put it, "straighten things up a bit" before her new help came on the scene. I could tell she was still not 100% OK with the deal I made with Laura.

Lacy and Lex came with her and immediately began to play with Oro, who was delighted with the company. Shortly after our initial greetings, I laid down some ground work that I hoped would start the arrangement off on the right foot.

"Laura, as you know, this old place is large and I'm almost certain you'll want to plan the cleaning over at least a two-day span. Lea will assist you with a work schedule and she's agreed to oversee the operation."

Lea began her role as Lady of the House and gave Laura a tour of the home. I simply followed along. She let Laura know that she preferred to clean the master bedroom and bath herself. With the instructions taken care of, Lea and I left for her apartment.

I was glad she had rented the place furnished, so we would not be hauling anything large like refrigerators, stoves or grand pianos. We managed to box up and load everything remaining in the apartment in one trip. That completed the task of relocating Lea's possessions to their new home at Rainbow Acres. Now she was faced with the chore of putting her things away.

Upon our return, I told Laura that she could schedule a thorough cleaning of the vacated apartment, even though

Lea said she could do it. Of course she could do it, but I didn't want her to waste her energy on that when there were more important things to take care of.

At home, Lea busied herself with moving her clothes and miscellaneous items into the master bedroom. By the time I had finished unloading the truck, Laura had completed the shelf cleaning in the study, so I made an effort to begin the task of properly arranging books on them from my own stack of boxes. Oro came in for a visit and a rest from the kids or maybe they were the ones who needed a rest from him.

"Will, do you ever look at any of those old books?" he asked.

"Well, to be truthful with you ... as if I could get away with lying to you ... I don't very often."

"Why, then ..."

I interrupted him with, "Oro, I have them because I like looking at them on the shelves and what is a study without lots of books?"

"It will look nice once you are done," he offered as if to appease me. *"At least Lea won't have to dust them, since you hired Laura. Before I forget it, Lex wants to ask you to attend some affair with Lacy and him. I'm not sure if he will have the nerve to ask you though."*

"What kind of an affair?"

"It's something to do with fathers being invited to school for breakfast. You do know, I'm sure, that he and the girl like you very much? You are their hero, I suppose, after what you did for them on Christmas Eve."

"Well, they are good kids and don't forget you were instrumental in the case too. I'll start up a conversation with him later to see if he comes out with whatever he wants me to do."

"There is something else that I picked up in a conversation between the children about school. Evidently, there is a boy named Bobby Rogers, who must be the resident bully. Lex normally takes his lunch to school and this kid, Bobby,

often takes Lex's chips or other food items. It's not exactly the crime of the century, but I thought I'd bring it up."

"Thanks, Oro. I'll have to throw that into my conversation with the boy and see where it leads."

I continued with my task at hand, while Oro lay down to nap. About an hour had passed when the children entered quietly and approached my desk. Lex reluctantly moved in front of Lacy and spoke.

"Mr. Jacobs, can I ask you a favor?"

"Of course Lex, what's on your mind?"

"At our school next week we are having 'Donuts for Dad's Day.' They do it every year and me and Lacy have never been able to go to it because our real dad is not around. Would you like to go and be our pretend dad?"

"Lex, I would be honored to accept your offer, as long as it's OK with your mother and it doesn't break any rules at school."

"You wouldn't break any rules. Some kids invite an uncle or grandpa. It just can't be a woman for this party."

Lacy jumped in with, "That's when the school does a 'Muffins for Mom's Day.' We have a mom, but we don't have a dad."

"OK, let's go find your mother and ask about her feelings on the subject."

Laura was not hard to track down; one only had to follow the sound of the vacuum. She was working on the third floor. At times, the trek to the top of the stairs winded me. Now that we were well into the winter months, I had not been doing much in the physical exercise department. Maybe I should take Lea's slick little hint and join The Fitness Center. Going to a public place to workout had never appealed to me before, but going with her might not be so bad. I made a mental note to myself to talk with her about the idea. Oro, who was trailing our little expedition, let me know that he was tuned in.

"Don't worry about forgetting the thought Will, I'll remind you. I have noticed that there are a few pounds around

your waistline that could be expended with a little work," he offered with a snicker.

"Thanks for noticing," I verbally replied.

"Thanks for noticing what, Mr. Jacobs?" Lacy asked.

"Oh, nothing, Sweety, I'm just talking to myself. It's something older people do a lot."

The top half-story of the house had not been previously used for anything other than an attic storage space. Lea and I thought it had a lot of potential to become a sunroom and observation area. The architect turned our ideas into plans and the contractors completed the transformation. We added windows all around and a sliding door on the backside, which opened outside onto a mini-deck and walk area that encompassed the room. It reminded me of a light house on the coast except that our lookout was square, not round. Maybe we should have added a multi-colored beacon on top of the house ... or not!

The elevation of the walkway around the third floor was just over the tops of the cedar trees that surrounded the house and the view, especially at dawn and dusk was often worth the trek up the stairs. We had done nothing in the way of furnishing the 500 square-foot room, but that would come in time. I even considered installing an elevator, for when I got older.

With an effort (on my part), we finally made it to the top landing. Laura turned off the noise maker when she saw us enter. The kids rapidly explained their request for my presence with them at school. She told them they should not have bothered me with the idea and began to apologize to me.

"I'm sorry, Mr. Jacobs. Please don't feel obligated to accept. They had no right to ask you in the first place."

"Laura, it's OK and please call me 'Will.' I'd love to go to school with them. I've never spent much time with elementary kids before and I rather enjoy the difference between them and those of high school age."

"I'll agree if you are sure you won't mind?" she said, "It is a big deal at their school. The kids get to show their parents their classroom and a special project that they do just for the occasion. I will be going with them next week on Thursday."

"I'll look forward to it. How are you coming along? Do you need anything?"

"No, thank you. I'm glad it's warmer today, so I can clean all the windows on the outside."

Laura and I talked for a few minutes longer about the house and told me I could meet the kids at their school on Wednesday morning at 7:00, or pick them up at her house around 6:30 a.m. The early hour was required so the little breakfast and open house for the dads could be concluded before the normal class starting time. I opted to pick them up at their house.

Laura, Lacy and Lex departed a little after six. I informed Lea of the arrangement I had made with the children. She praised me for my involvement.

"Will, that is such a nice gesture and I'm sure the kids are thrilled that you accepted."

"I don't know about 'thrilled', but they seemed pleased. I've often wondered what sort of a father I would be and even briefly fantasized about having a son or daughter. I might emphasize the word 'briefly.'"

"We never have discussed the subject of kids after we are married," said Lea quietly.

"I guess we haven't. Do you want children, Doe?"

"I am not able to have any of my own. I had medical problems when I was nineteen and complications put an end to the possibility."

"I'm sorry, Lea, I didn't know. I know you mentioned that you've been married, but I could tell you didn't want to talk about it."

"Yes, I was married right out of high school. My boyfriend and I eloped. The parents, on both sides, were against the bond and wanted us to get through college first. I wish I had listened to them. Young people usually aren't mature enough to take on the commitment. My own marriage lasted less than a year."

We dropped the subject.

Wednesday rolled around and I arrived at Laura's home to transport the kids to school and participate in the early morning frivolities. The time began with an adequate breakfast, but nothing compared to Lea's, except for maybe the "Krispy Kream" donuts. Now remember, I have always contended that her home made cinnamon rolls were "to die for", but there was something almost spiritual about these donuts, since they were almost too good to have been made in this world.

After the light meal, the kids took me on a short tour of the school and their individual classrooms, where the students had posted their most recent art work all over the walls. The theme was for Valentine's Day. Lacy had even taken the time to draw a "Be my Valentine" picture for me, which made me quite pleased. She was a darling of a young girl, petite in size, quiet in manner and always polite. She had long, light-brown hair and adorable green eyes.

"Say kids, an interesting thought crossed my mind this morning on my way to pick you up. Your mom's initials are 'L. L.' as are yours. I'm curious. What are your middle names?"

Lacy answered the question. "Our middle names are the same, but spelled different. Mine is 'L-E-A' and Lex's is 'L-E-E'."

"That's ironic. Did you mention it to "my" Lea while you were at the house last weekend?"

"No," she answered, "we didn't talk to her much."

"Well, I think that will change. She was very busy with the tasks of organizing her things that we brought over from her apartment. I'm sure we will all become good friends, since you will probably be coming to visit when your mom is working at our house."

At that moment, a friend of Lacy's came up to her and the two left together to head for their classroom. Lex and I remained in the hallway and I decided to ask him about what Oro had previously overheard a few days before.

"Lex, I want to discuss another matter with you. Who is Bobby Rogers?"

He paused, as his eyes widened and he looked slightly confused, but he answered with, "Uh, he's a kid in my fifth grade class."

"I've heard rumors that he takes things from you."

"Do you mean my money?"

"I heard he takes part of your lunch. Does he take your money, too?"

Lex must have been puzzled at how I knew about Bobby, but he continued without asking me any questions. "Sometimes. If I have money he might take it and if he likes anything in my lunch he takes whatever he wants. The same thing happens to some of my friends."

"Why don't you and your friends tell your teacher about what is going on?"

"Bobby has told us that he will 'beat us to a pulp' if we do. I haven't told my mom, either."

"Well, that's going to stop, I promise you. Is he here this morning with his father?"

"I haven't seen him, but he will prob'bly be here later, when school really starts."

I pulled out my wallet, found Captain Rigley's business card and handed it to the boy.

"Lex, I want you to give this card to Bobby when you see him. Will you do that?" He looked at the card and nodded in agreement. "Tell him if he tries to take anything from you or any of the other students he will be having a meeting with this police officer, the principal and his parents."

"Wow! You can get the cops to make him quit bothering me and the other kids?"

"I certainly can. Oro and I have been working with the police department on solving crime and Captain Rigley is a friend of ours." I started to leave, but Lex reached out and took hold of my arm.

"Mr. Jacobs, thank you very much for coming to the breakfast for me and Lacy ... and thank you also for helping me with Bobby. I wish you were my real dad because you are a nice man and we all like you very much."

"Well, Lex ... maybe you and Lacy can adopt me for your pretend dad, like you said before. I will be around for both of you, whenever you need me."

"If we knew how to adopt you, we would do that."

"Let's just say it's a done deal; like a pact. We can seal the contract with a handshake," I replied as I held out my hand to the boy.

"Awesome," Lex said, and his small hand disappeared inside the grasp of mine. "I can't wait until I tell Lacy and Mom."

"Ahhh ... Lex, can you let me explain our agreement to your mother first?"

"Oh, sure, but I know she will be happy about it too. I already told you that we all like you very much."

"Yes, I know and I like you all, as well. Tell your mother I will call her this evening."

"I will. Good bye ... Dad!!!"

A lump formed in my throat, but I managed to reply, "Thank you, Lex. Good bye for now." I was emotionally moved by his simple statement and suddenly felt a little unfulfilled in life. I probably would never be a true dad, but I could at least partially play the role in the future.

CHAPTER 8

DISCOVERY IN THE COUNTRY

DEAR, YOU HAVEN'T TAKEN ME OUT TO EAT FOR AWHILE NOW, SO LET'S GO SOMEWHERE."

"I'M SORRY I HAVE BEEN SO NEGLECTFUL, DOE. WHERE WOULD YOU LIKE TO GO?"

"I RAN ACROSS A DISCOUNT COUPON IN THE PAPER FOR THE CARRIAGE HOUSE IN YODER. LET'S GO THERE."

"I'D SECOND THAT MOTION. IT'S BEEN QUITE AWHILE SINCE I'VE EATEN THERE AND WE'VE NEVER BEEN THERE TOGETHER. WE SHOULD LEAVE FAIRLY SOON TO ARRIVE BEFORE THE EVENING CROWD, ESPECIALLY SINCE IT WILL TAKE ABOUT HALF AND HOUR TO GET THERE.

SHORTLY AFTER OUR ARRIVAL IN YODER, A DELICIOUS OLD STYLE, ALL-YOU-CAN-EAT MEAL WAS SOON FORTHCOMING. MOST WOULD CALL THE COMMUNITY A MERE "WIDE SPOT IN THE ROAD", BUT THE CALM, SERENE ATMOSPHERE OF THE SMALL BERG WAS REFRESHING.

WE DECIDED TO RETURN HOME BY A ROUNDABOUT WAY TO AVOID THE ORDEAL OF FACING HEAVY TRAFFIC CONGESTION IF WE TOOK THE SHORTEST ROUTE. I BYPASSED THE HIGHWAY AND HEADED DIRECTLY SOUTH ON THE MAIN BLACKTOP ROAD THAT RAN THROUGH YODER.

THE ROUTE SOON TURNED INTO A TYPICAL RURAL KANSAS ROAD THAT CONSISTED OF A MIXTURE OF DIRT, SAND AND GRAVEL. THE CHANGE IN SURFACE CONDITIONS REQUIRED A REDUCED SPEED, BUT WE ALL ENJOYED THE SCENERY FROM THE SLOWER PACE. AS I DROVE BY AN OPENING IN THE THICK ROW OF OSAGE ORANGE trees, I caught a brief glimpse of a horse and buggy in front of an interesting structure.

Many of the original settlers and farmers, who laid claim to large areas of Kansas, had planted trees, commonly called "hedge trees" in rows to eventually "fence" off parts of the land into one-square-mile sections.

Something, an impulsive feeling maybe, made me stop, turn the Jeep around and return to the narrow drive. What we found on the other side of the trees was a small church, built of uneven sizes of stone blocks and back dropped by a dense grove of evergreens. Boston ivy had consumed the church building on its north side and was progressively advancing over the roof and walls to the south.

In front, tied to a long, wooden rail was a tall and stately looking shiny, jet black horse hitched to an old black buggy. I knew the residents in this part of Kansas were predominately Amish, whose culture and background was one of great interest and even mystery to many people, including me.

I parked alongside, but not too close to the horse that wore black curved blinders attached to its bridle. They are used to block the animal's peripheral vision, but he turned his head full to the right and looked at us with interest. Oro returned the intent stare. The nostrils of the horse flared wide in an attempt to catch a whiff of Oro, whose tail was actively beating the back and sides of the Jeep's interior. We remained in the vehicle for a few moments, before Lea spoke, almost in a whisper.

"Will, I must see inside."

We left the vehicle, strolled up the flagstone walk to the large double doors and knocked. A middle-aged woman soon opened one side and greeted us amiably.

"Good morning, I'm Elsa. May I help you?" She wore the normal attire for Amish females, a near floor length solid black dress and matching head scarf.

"Elsa, could we come in and look at your church?" Lea asked.

"Oh, it's not my church, Ma'am, but you are welcome to look around. I work here to keep the place nice and tidy for the preacher.

Lea and I followed the woman inside. Oro, who didn't need to be told, stayed outside. He mentioned his desire to meet the horse "up close and personal." I mentally reminded him to stay out from behind him.

We learned from Elsa that the country church was non-denominational. I hadn't realized it, but different orders of the Amish don't typically have established churches. The more devout members spread the worship around to individual homes of the families in any given area.

Once inside, the woman shut the door behind us and we were engulfed in near darkness. Our eyes would need to adjust from being outside in the light, but there was another reason for the drastic change in visibility. It was soon evident that the interior of the building had no electric lighting. It was a few minutes before we could properly admire our surroundings. Only a few of the numerous candles that lined the outside walls and railings had been lit.

Everything, from top to bottom, was constructed of wood or different types of stone. All the work, of course, was done by hand. The ceiling was a series of exposed pine logs used for beams and trusses and was very impressive. The floor was a continuation of the same flat stone from outside the walk and landing. The posts at the end of the each pew were ornately hand carved. The aisle was centered between two small sections of seating and led to a raised altar. The length of the room ended with an immense fireplace, whose size would rival the one back at Rainbow Acres.

Lea asked Elsa for the name and contact information for the preacher of the church and we ended our short tour of the facility. We returned to the bright outdoors and Lea was outwardly excited.

"Dear, we must have our wedding here. I know it is small, but that should not be a major problem. If we select only our closest family and best friends, I am sure there will be ample room inside. The whole place is just sooooo lovely and quaint. What do you think?"

"I think you need to take a breath, Doe. Actually, I was tossing the idea around in the 'ole gray matter myself, but thought the size of the church was smaller than you would want. Since you've already taken that aspect into consideration, I guess we should see if it's available to outside folk."

We loved the tranquility of the place and how it was isolated from the noise and fast-paced atmosphere of the city. When we left the church, Lea instructed me to drive back to Yoder, where the pastor lived. With the accurate directions provided by Elsa, we found him quite easily, learned what we needed to know and reserved the church for our July wedding.

Chapter 9

A Request from Rigley

CAPTAIN RIGLEY PHONED me shortly before noon, seemingly to shoot the breeze, but I knew there had to be more to the call. He was not the type of person to expend energy on idle gossip or small talk without a purpose. Oro and I had been "conversing" about one thing or another and his ears perked up when he heard me mention the Captain's name. Rigley spoke casually for only a brief period before getting to why he had really called.

"While I've got you on the line, I have an offer to make you."

I knew it. The call was not just a friendly one. I hadn't known him for long, but I could already read him like a book.

"OK, what is it?"

"First off, I've probably not thanked you properly in the past for your help, but I do appreciate your previous assistance and I would like to utilize your talents in the future."

"Well, you're entirely welcome. The experiences have been rewarding to us too."

"Us? Oh yes, you and the dog. In fact, what I have to offer you includes your hound."

"Really? I'm even more interested now."

"There is an area K-9 training course beginning the first of next month and I'd like to know if you cared to attend? The department would pick up the fee for the class."

"Now that is ironic, because I asked Oro, the day we searched for the girl, if he wanted to go to some type of training school."

Oro quickly jumped in with, "*Will, do you know what you just said?*"

"Is that right?" responded Rigley. "And what did he say?"

"Uh, nothing of course, since he's a dog, but I'm sure he would enjoy it," I said as I gave Oro a wink.

"Whatever," Rigley said. "Anyway I want you to be on the force in a support role and with the training you could be on a case without me having to explain your presence."

"Have you been taking some heat because of us?"

"Only a little from my chief, who may have received complaints or concerns from others, but I won't have any problems if you could do the class."

"How long does it last?"

"It's only a three-day course."

"Well, Oro and I can easily do that. It's not like we are overly busy with any projects at the present time."

"Good, I'll get you signed up and check back with you on the particulars."

He hung up without saying "good-bye", as usual. One of these days I was going to bring up the subject of phone etiquette to him.

Oro began dancing around the room, in a peculiar fashion. Since Rigley was a loud talker, he already heard the full conversation about the class.

"*That's awesome news, Will.*"

"Sounds like it, Oro. Let's go tell Lea."

Lea was in the kitchen fixing us a light lunch. I told her of Rigley's request to send me to the three day police K-9 handler class with Oro.

"I don't believe that will keep you two out of trouble for very long, but I'm sure that you will enjoy yourselves."

The very next morning a patrol car pulled up in front of the house and Officer Margaret emerged. Oro and I had been out checking the Fleetwood Eagle that was housed inside the barn and we greeted her in the drive. She handed me a notebook and an envelope.

Her only words were, "Captain Rigley asked me to drop this off."

I thanked her and she left. As we headed for the house, I looked at the three inch notebook. It was titled "K-9 Training Manual" and inside the envelope was a newsletter about a three-day course for recertification. I went straight to the phone and called Rigley.

"Captain, this is Will Jacobs and I have a question about the information your officer brought me just a few minutes ago."

"What about it?"

"The class Oro and I are attending is a recertification class. We haven't been certified, as you very well know, so what's the deal?"

"Jacobs, it just so happens that I have a copy of you and your dog's certification right here in front of me. Is there a problem?"

"I see ... but how can we ..."

"That's why I sent you the manual. You've got a couple of weeks to catch up on what you need to know before class. I gotta go," he said and the line went dead.

"Well, at least he sort of said good bye," I commented to Oro. "Boy, we've got work to do."

"I'm ready, willing and able."

"We need to look this manual over to see what we've gotten ourselves into, big guy. We have a couple of weeks to prepare for a retest of what most teams would learn after maybe an eight-week course."

"Don't worry, Will. We don't have much on our plate, as you like to say, so we should do fine with the time we do have."

Oro followed me into the study and plopped down beside the recliner I had chosen to occupy. I first reviewed the chapters in the course book on how to become a K-9 Team. After a few minutes, I gave an overview of the course to Oro.

"There's quite a bit of classroom and study work to do, which is bound to be boring, but some of the other things might turn out to be fun, like a few of the outdoor practical exercises. There's also a section about a water and land obstacle course that each dog must go through. A pool is used for the course described for the water exercise. I'm sure you could easily pass that part."

"I hope it's an indoor pool, because the water temperature in our pond is still really cold."

"That explains why you haven't gone for a swim for quite some time. For the land course, I could set up a similar one in the back yard for you to practice with."

"That may be a good idea, since I'm probably a little out of shape with all the lounging around we've been doing this past winter."

"I can relate to that, boy. Lea still hints to me that I'm welcome to join her at the fitness center she's been going to since last fall. I know I'd better drop a few pounds before the wedding."

"Only a few?"

"Hey, watch your mouth, Oro." He responded only with a laugh. "OK, I'll make a list of some materials I'll need to construct some sort of course and then we'll head out for Lowes."

"When it's finished, Jay Jay and I can practice on it together."

We completed our purchasing trip and were within a few hundred yards of Rainbow Acres when it became evident that a vehicle was pulled off to the side of the road near our driveway.

"Will, I see people inside the car. Are you going to stop to investigate?"

"Yes, I probably should."

I drove passed our entryway a short distance and pulled up beside an unfamiliar, dark blue, older model

Ford Mustang. As I came to a stop alongside, I leaned ahead of Oro (he prefers to sit in the front passenger seat) to speak to the driver within; a woman, who was talking on a cell phone.

"Hello, do you need assistance?"

"Hold on a minute, someone's here," she said to whomever she was talking to and turned to look over at us. "As a matter of fact we do."

The "we" consisted of herself and a young girl passenger, who I assumed was the woman's daughter.

"What's the trouble?"

"We're out of gas."

"We live right here," I said as I pointed in the direction of the house. My gas cans are actually empty, but I'd be happy to go into the station to get one filled for you."

"Could you? I'd be so grateful. My husband can't leave work just now and our only alternatives are to call a tow truck or take off walking. If I'd have signed up for a Triple-A membership, they'd have brought me gas by now."

"That's true. We are members and their services are great. In the meantime, I'll get a can and be right back."

Oro offered to stay at home while I did the neighborly thing to help the two, but I wanted him to come along. When we returned, the pair had left the car and were standing by our mail box. The woman raised her hand to stop me as we approached.

"I hate to impose," she began, "but could we go with you? I'm not really comfortable sitting out here; stranded in the middle of nowhere."

"Sure. We are a little off the beaten path. Hop in," I said as I hit the unlock button on the panel in the armrest.

"My name's Will and my companion here is Oro."

Without being asked, Oro had jumped into the back seat. I raised the center console to its up position to make room for the company.

"Can I ride shotgun?" the girl asked, as she stood in the doorway, looking at me.

"I haven't heard that expression for quite a while. I don't care if your mother doesn't mind."

"Mom?"

"I suppose."

"Sweeet," the girl remarked as she moved out of the way to let her mother get in first to occupy the middle spot.

"Thank you, ah, Will. I'm Claudia and this is my daughter, Brittany."

"The closest gas station is in Clearwater, so it won't take too long."

"If you're going that way, maybe you could do me another favor and drop Brit off at Starwood's Outdoor Education Center. She's almost late for a day camp training session being held there."

"No problem. I know right where that is. In fact, I've given a few talks to some groups of girls there about becoming an author."

"Hey! Brit exclaimed, "That's what I want to be. I'm writing a story about a little girl and her dog."

"Now, that's interesting, Brittany. I could look at it, if you'd like and critique it for you."

"Oh, sweeeeet, Mr. uh …"

"It's Jacobs, but …"

The woman interrupted with, "Brit, Honey, I don't believe the writing in that journal of yours is ready to be read by anyone."

The oral conversation subsided at that point and Oro cued me.

"I could catch you up on some late breaking news, if you are interested."

I was, so I simply nodded my head.

"She's thankful that we came along when we did and that you weren't a 'sicko'. I guess her imagination must have been getting the best of her, because she was concerned with their safety. I also know from her that the husband had refused to help them and I believe they are separated and in the process of getting a divorce."

Oro paused, as if to give me time to digest the information he had given and then continued.

"I learned, from Brittany, that she's really interested in writing, but her mother doesn't take her serious, since she's only a fifth grader. She wishes her mom would let her attend one of Wichita's literary magnet schools next fall that concentrates on reading and writing."

We arrived at Starwood's and the Camp Ranger directed us to the drop off area, away from the main parking lot. Brit departed and we continued down the country road to the gas station on the outskirts of Clearwater, a small, rural community southwest of Wichita. I filled up three two-gallon cans and the truck before heading back for home.

Claudia must have been in her early 30's. She was tall, maybe 5' 11" tall and slender. I pegged her as being a runner and basketball star during her high school and/or college years. Talk between us on the way back was minimal. I did state to her that I was an author and writer and was honestly interested in helping Brittany with her writing. I gave her my card, but not much was exchanged from her verbally, except for a thank you, after I put the gas from one of the cans into her car. She tried to pay me, but I told her the rule of being a Good Samaritan is to do something nice for someone else. This will repay the kindness one receives from another. OK, I probably made it up, but I believe in the principle of the gesture.

It was now time to take care of business at home and construct an obstacle course for Oro.

CHAPTER 10

K-9 TRAINING

THE POLICE K-9 Handler & Dog Recertification Course began "bright and early", as is often said. It was certainly not bright outside, but it was early, because the starting time for the class was six a.m. There were ten teams of human and canine partners enrolled. Oro looked out of place, for he was of a non-traditional breed and the only dog present with a light-colored coat. Rottweilers, shepherds and Dobermans filled out the rest of the spots of his species. Oro and I were also bound to be the only duo not working for some branch of law enforcement.

All but one of the people in attendance wore some type of outerwear that depicted their affiliation. Rigley had, at least, thought to give me a jacket with his police department's logo stenciled on the breast pocket, so we looked somewhat official.

The first part of the class agenda was designated as "Meet and Greet". The human participants, nine men and one woman, took turns introducing themselves and their canine partners, along with a short bio, to the rest of the group. I was impressed with some of the credentials told to us by several in the class.

When my turn came, I simply mentioned of my support status with the local department and gave Oro the credit due him for saving a boy from drowning last summer while we were in Colorado. The information I shared elevated Oro's status among the group and I could tell he was pleased and equally proud of his accomplishment. I was looking forward to this summer's return to the Lake

City area, where Oro was to be honored for his deed in a planned ceremony. The boy he saved just happened to be the son of a very influential resident of the town.

Oro came across with, "*Will, the man next to us, who didn't mention who he worked for, must be with the CIA or some other hush-hush branch of the government, because he has been thinking about his workload back at the 'agency'. His name, by the way, is not Bob Simms either. It's Tony.*"

The individual happened to be the lone person not wearing some type of identifying attire. After introductions had concluded, we reassembled outside. The itinerary showed us reviewing our verbal and silent commands before agility training. Paul, our instructor, was a fellow of about fifty who was small in stature, but not in voice. He must have been a marine drill sergeant at one time in his career.

He instructed us to line up along a fence line with about ten feet between each team. We handlers were told to separate ourselves from our dogs in another line about twenty paces away.

Paul stood behind the row of dogs and held up cards to denote which silent signal he wanted us to relay to our partner. Each of us in turn followed his direction until all the dogs were now sitting at our right side because the last two signals given each dog were "come" and "heel". This brought all the dogs from the fence line to our positions.

Paul asked the "mystery handler", Bob (aka Tony), to repeat the silent commands according to how the manual illustrated them. Bob had given his dog, Sam, signals other than what was prescribed for in the text. After Bob and Sam repeated the exercise properly, Paul addressed us.

"You may improvise and even add hand commands with your dog, but the required signs are mandatory. What if you were incapacitated for any reason at the scene? One of your fellow officers may need to communicate a command to your dog. It could lead to problems if your

K9 is taught different signs than those that are depicted in the manual.

During the vocal command segment, Bob gave his orders in German. I guess he didn't want anyone else to order his dog around. He and Sam happened to be positioned next to us, so during our break I decided to give him something to think about.

"Hey Tony, why do you speak to Sam, if that is his real name, in German?"

From the look of surprise on his face, using his actual name in the question had obviously stunned him. He studied me for a moment before answering.

"My name is Bob and my dog's name is Sam."

"OK, so Bob, why are your commands in German?"

"Because he's a German shepherd."

"Well, that only makes sense, I suppose," I said with a smile. "What branch of law enforcement are you with?"

"That isn't important."

Oro had been doing his thing and decided to update me.

"Tony is an agent with the NSA and he's upset that you know his real name."

I would have let the subject die, but the guy had a cocky attitude about him. I decided to further his bewilderment.

"OK then, if I have to guess, I'd say you must be an agent with the NSA."

Again, my comment set him back and he gave me another intent look. I chose not to bother him anymore and ended the conversation by walking off with Oro. My decision coincided with the group being directed to move across a field to the Canine Agility Course.

This was, for the most part, a treat for Oro. He enjoyed going through and over culvert pipes, negotiating a series of mazes and dashing around most of the obstacle course. The hardest task he faced was climbing a modified stepladder to a platform about ten feet off the ground. I urged him on as he began to falter about half way up the narrow steps of the ladder. Oro, being quite long and tall, was having a difficult time and his back legs began to shake. He was about to loose his balance and opted to jump off the side where he landed awkwardly on the ground with a resounding "thud".

"*Will*," he relayed to me with a groan, "*I wasn't able to practice this skill at home. Can I give it another shot?*"

"That's OK, boy. Try it again if you want too, but be careful."

He did and with great determination was able to make it to the platform, but now all four legs seemed to be shaking uncontrollably. I told him to relax before trying to accomplish the next feat, which was crossing over to another platform on a four-inch beam of about twenty feet in length. Oro sat down and regained some of his composure before attempting to cross the beam. I would never forgive myself if he fell off and broke a leg or worse and positioned myself under him just in case of an accident. He proceeded slowly with concentration and made it with no further difficulty. The descent on the other side consisted of a series of normal steps and landings, which he did easily.

"*Whew*," he expressed to me after returning to the ground. "*I hope I don't have to do that very often.*"

"You did great Oro. I'm sorry, I must have overlooked that part of the training in the book."

I'm sure he felt better when three other dogs were unable to negotiate the exercise. His favorite part of the day was at the water hazard training that consisted of an obstacle course set up in and around an indoor pool. Several objects had been placed in the water that had to either be avoided or climbed over and during three segments of the course the dogs had to jump off raised platforms of varying heights into the pool. Oro was in his element and easily outclassed the other participants.

After the exercise concluded, we dried our animals, received a list of scenarios to take with us for human homework and were dismissed for the day. Oro and I were about to depart when Bob and Sam came up to us.

"Will," Bob began, "I should apologize for my attitude towards you earlier today. I'm not having a very good year so far, but that's no excuse for being rude to you."

"It's OK, Bob. I shouldn't have played mind games with you. Let's consider it behind us and make a new start tomorrow."

"That's fine with me," he said, as he looked around as if to check that we weren't being overheard. "I would, however, like to know how you knew my real name and where I worked?"

"Well, let's just say I have my sources, who must remain anonymous."

"Fine, but I'd appreciate it if you would keep the information to yourself. My specific employment and personal data is not supposed to be public knowledge."

"I understand Bob and I promise to be more discreet in the future."

With that settled and after a handshake, we both left for the parking lot.

"*Will,*" Oro began, "*do you feel that we did a decent job today?*"

"I think you did a superb job through all of the tasks ... even on the ladder, which I could see was not easy for any of the dogs, but do you think our efforts here are worth the time?

"*Of course it is. I have really looked forward to attending the class and I'm not at all disappointed. I like a challenge and so far it has been a personally rewarding experience. I could sense from the other K-9's involved that they do the work partly to please their handlers, but they enjoy it too. Will, do you wish you had not accepted the captain's request?*"

"I did when I was afraid you were going to break your neck on the ladder and beam, but I guess I'm glad we got involved."

"*Remember when Bob said he was not having a very good year?*"

"Yes, did you pick up any reasons why?"

"*It sounds like he and Sam will be going to the Middle East soon to search out terrorists. He's not afraid of going, but his wife wants him to quit his job and stay home.*"

"I can certainly understand her feelings. This may be one case that we have no control over and I don't know how we could help."

"*I suppose you're right,*" was Oro's reply, as we began our drive back to Rainbow Acres.

Once home, Oro and I (mostly I) informed Lea of how our day had gone and then I started on the homework. It consisted of reading a series of scenarios that a handler and his K9 partner may face during any number of police confrontations with the criminal element and other situations, such as crowd control.

Questions followed each case and the answers were generally common sense, with the main emphasis always being on the side of safety for the officer, his fellow officers (including his dog) and the public at large. Little was mentioned about the bad guys except for the concern that law enforcement should refrain from using excessive force.

We started off the second day on an interesting note, by going over some of the homework at the beginning of class. This lasted until our first break at nine, but the rest of the day was basically filled with I-wish-I-were-not-here tasks. Instruction involved the medical portion of the training update. We underwent infant, child and adult CPR training, to maintain certification in those tasks, as well as reviews over the ABC's of patient assessment and care. Regular first aid treatment and procedures were thrown in for added "excitement." I'd be one of the first to admit that medical training is important, but not a particularly interesting subject.

I was one of several teachers designated to obtain and maintain a First Responder level of medical training. I was selected, because I was already certified through my duties as a volunteer firefighter. I'll have to admit that the training has been of value occasionally, but that didn't make those classes any less boring.

Fortunately the medical instruction was broken up by several practical applications of what the homework had gone over. Our K9 teams were able to conduct area and room-to-room searches of different structures on the grounds, which included an actual two-story home, a warehouse and even replicas of a strip mall and a school, both of which were used for mock hostage taking scenarios.

After a long, twelve hour day, I was beat mentally, but Oro was in good spirits and even managed a sense of humor.

"I was happy to be a dog through most of that first aid talk and I know how much you were dreading it. Many of those lectures made for easy nap times, like golf on the tube does for you."

"That's a good observation and comparison, Oro."

The third day was the most enjoyable of the course. In the morning, we handlers had to re-qualify in the use of various weapons. I was not that experienced with hand guns, but held my own at the outdoor target range. It was also critical to make sure that the dogs were comfortable with the sounds from the firing of weapons.

In the afternoon we were put in the field or more accurately, in the forest, in a search for several "escaped" convicts, who were hiding somewhere in over two hundred acres of heavily wooded area.

In the search, Oro received praises from our instructor for spotting a man who had climbed a tree and was about thirty feet off the ground. I told Paul that Oro had come on point and had continued to bark at the guy until I realized why he was barking. In actuality, Oro had notified me that he saw the guy in the tree, so I told him to bark. Evidently, the staff member had never been found in the tree before, by any of the other classes that he had been a part of.

Training lasted into the evening and we all were getting rather hungry, since only donuts in the morning and assorted sandwiches at lunch had been provided. Oro and I were both relieved when certificates of completion were handed out to the class and we were permitted to leave. One team did not successfully complete the recertification training.

Lea was surprised that we were so late in returning, but willingly warmed up leftovers for me. Oro and I again critiqued our day for her and we both were praised for our accomplishments in the course.

CHAPTER 11

ORO'S NEW FRIEND

ORO AND I WERE TAKING IT EASY IN THE STUDY. LEA CAME TO THE DOORWAY, BUT DID NOT ENTER. SHE SURVEYED THE SCENE WITHIN. ORO WAS SACKED OUT ON HIS FAVORITE RESTING PLACE, A THICK PAD OF SADDLE BLANKETS AND I WAS AT THE COMPUTER WORKING ON MY NEXT COLUMN OF "GRIZZLY'S THIS 'N THAT" FOR FRIDAY'S EDITION OF <u>THE HAYSVILLE TIMES</u>.

"DEAR, I'M GOING TO RUN OVER TO THE MARKET FOR A FEW THINGS."

"YOU'D GET THERE AND BACK FASTER IF YOU DROVE THE JEEP, DOE."

"HA, HA. WHAT A FUNNY BOY YOU ARE TODAY. DID YOU DREAM LAST NIGHT THAT YOU WERE A COMEDIAN?"

"SAY, THAT'S A GOOD ONE."

"DO YOU WANT ME TO PICK UP ANYTHING FOR YOU?"

"NO, I CAN'T THINK OF ANYTHING, UNLESS IT WOULD BE A SNICKER'S BAR."

"I WILL BUY YOU A SNICKER'S, BUT YOU WILL HAVE TO PULL A 'HONEY DO' TO GET IT."

ABOUT A MONTH AGO, WE (MOSTLY LEA) MADE A GAME OUT OF HOUSEHOLD CHORES. LEA WROTE LOW PRIORITY TASKS DOWN ON NOTES AND PLACED THE SLIPS OF PAPER IN AN ANTIQUE COOKIE JAR. AT VARIOUS TIMES DURING THE WEEK AND ALWAYS ON A SATURDAY MORNING, I WOULD PULL A NOTE FROM THE JAR. WHATEVER JOB I PICKED, WOULD BE ONE OF MY PROJECTS FOR THE DAY.

"I CAN DO THAT, DOE, BUT I HOPE I DON'T SELECT THE 'PAINT THE HOUSE' SLIP."

WITH THE AWARD OF A CANDY BAR IN EXCHANGE FOR A FAVOR AGREED UPON, SHE DEPARTED. I WENT BACK TO ADD A FEW MORE words to my column and Oro resumed his dreams about chasing rabbits in the field, squirrels in the yard or ducks on the pond.

Lea had been gone about an hour, when Oro raised up from his bed.

"Will, we have company."

I was facing the window, which looked out towards the entry drive, but had seen no one pull up and shared my observations with Oro.

"I didn't hear a car, but I'm sure I heard a dog bark in the back yard."

"I didn't hear anything, but we had better check it out. I know your senses are keener than mine, but you may have been dreaming."

Before we made it through the kitchen, a light tapping on the mudroom door was heard. Within moments I reached the door and opened it to find a young girl standing on the back porch. Beside her was a large black lab, with a panting tongue at the front end and a wagging tail at the back. Even though the girl was standing and the dog was sitting, they were the same height.

"Well, good morning young lady and what can we do for you?"

"Hello, my name is Kayla Wilson and this is my dog, Jay Jay. We are your neighbors from across the hay field," said the young girl, as she pointed over her shoulder towards the northwest.

"Oh, do you live in the big yellow house?"

"Yes, that's the one. Me and Jay Jay were out for a walk and decided to come over for a visit."

"Well, that was nice of you."

I stepped outside to join them and introduced Oro to the girl and the dog. I sat down on the steps and she took a seat as well.

"Oh, we already know him from before, but I didn't know his name. I called him 'Old Yeller', 'cause I thought it was a good name for him."

"Really? Well, Oro didn't tell me you had been over."

Kayla laughed at my comment as I "heard" from Oro.

"Guess I forgot to tell you about their visit the other day when you took off and left me here."

I wondered about when that could have been. It's not often that I leave home without taking him with me. They must have come over when I went into town to the doctor's office for my yearly physical. I thought it would be too hot to leave him in the truck.

I picked up a tennis ball left beside the door and gave it a toss. Oro and his new friend charged after it and were soon involved in a serious game of chase.

"Do your folks know you are here, because they may be concerned with you visiting a stranger?"

"Oh, you're not really a stranger. My dad knows all about you and how you are rich 'n all. In fact, me and Jay Jay have walked over a few times to meet you, but you and Yeller, oops, I mean Oro, were always gone except for that one day when he was here and today, of course. I usually ask my brother to come with us, but he won't. He doesn't have time to have fun anymore. I didn't ask him today, 'cause his afternoon chores aren't done. He still had to feed the horses and stuff, when we left. I feed and water our chickens and collect the eggs. I did my work, so I could come over and here we are."

"Whew, catch a breath, little one. By the way, my fiancé, Lea, lives here too and I'm sorry that we have always been gone. Maybe I should give you our phone number and then you wouldn't have to make the long walk across the field for nothing."

"Oh, we don't really mind. Goin' for a hike and s'ploring is fun."

"Are your parents home now?"

"No, my mom doesn't live with us anymore and my dad is at my Uncle Robert's farm. He is helping him fix a tractor. My dad fixes lots of things. He won't be home 'till supper prob'bly, but my brother's still home, I guess."

"Well, Lea should be back any time now. Would you like to stick around for awhile to meet her?"

"Sure, me and Jay Jay are in no hurry. We can wait."

"Great. I take it that your dad farms, too?"

"Yes and us kids help him, when we are told to."

"Well, there's a lot to do on a farm. So, what grade are you in?"

"I'm in the fourth grade now and will be in the fifth grade after this summer is over."

"Well, that makes sense. Is your brother still in school?"

"Yeah, he's in high school. He knows your soon-to-be wife, but he's a senior, so doesn't have her as a teacher. I hope that she's my English teacher when I go to high school. I heard my brother say that she was the prettiest teacher in the whole school."

Oro came trotting back to us with Jay Jay at his side. He informed me that Lea was back.

"I'd have to agree with him about her being pretty. Actually, I believe my lovely lady has arrived."

At that moment the Wrangler came into view as it pulled around the corner of the house and stopped alongside the sidewalk to the steps. Lea exited the vehicle with a wave and a questioning look on her smiling face.

"Hello Dear. I see we have company ... how nice."

"Yes, we do."

I introduced our young visitor and her dog and added, "Kayla, I didn't catch your brother's name."

"Oh, it's Matt and it's short for Matthew, but he doesn't like his real name.

I filled Lea in on other information I had learned earlier, while she put me to work carrying a number of bags of groceries from the Jeep to the kitchen. We invited Kayla into the house to sample some cookies made the previous evening.

"Will, do you want to pull a note now or later?"

"I'll pull one later, thank you. Right now I'm going to take the dogs out for a stroll around the place."

They both had taken up positions on either side of Kayla and patiently assumed the role of beggars, but they were being quiet and calm about it.

I went to the cupboard, grabbed a handful of mini, look-a-like dog-bone treats and easily managed to entice the two tail-wagging canines to follow me outside. In short order they devoured what I had, so I told them to "go play."

Oro and Jay Jay began to romp around in the plush grass of the front yard. I sat on the porch swing and relaxed in the shade. Watching them play the way dogs do was such a pleasing sight. As Oro's only companion, I was not a suitable substitute to another big dog. I could provide him with all the exercise he needed in our games of fetch, but I could tell he was having more fun with Jay Jay. After Oro and his new friend had chased each other back and forth for quite some time they came up to me. They both were panting heavily and plopped down on the large doormats by the porch swing and front door.

"Will," Oro passed on to me, "*now that we know Jay Jay, can we visit each other?*"

"I don't know. I will check with Kayla's dad to see what he thinks about the idea, but I'm sure it will be OK to visit on a regular basis. Lea mentioned earlier that we should drive Kayla home to officially meet her family."

"*Kayla is very nice, but I have the feeling that her brother is not as happy as she is.*"

"Why do you say that? Was there something about him that you picked up from her?

Before Oro was able to respond, Lea summoned me with a call from the back door. I had been programmed well, because I simply yelled back that I was coming. I left the dogs outside, entered the front of the house and proceeded to the kitchen, where Lea met me. Kayla was seated at the large oak table and had finished her snack of milk and cookies. The table and chairs loomed even larger than in real life, when framed around the small, petite features of the young girl.

"Will, Kayla gave me her phone number, so I called. Her brother is home and said he could come over to pick up Kayla or we could bring her over and stay to wait for their dad, who had called earlier to say that he would be home soon to start supper."

"Kayla," I said, "I hope you don't get into hot water for coming over without letting your father know where you were."

"It's no big deal, Mr. Jacobs, 'cause I take off all the time. I would only be in trouble if I didn't do my chores first. I get really bored at home and me and Jay Jay take long walks together or sometimes I ride my bike to the Westside Mall to meet my best friend, Shelby. She's in my 4th grade class and lives near the mall."

"Oh, my goodness, Will, that's miles from here and across two major roadways. Kayla, does your father know you go that far away."

"I'm sure he does 'cause I tell him where I went when I get home."

"All right, let me get this kitchen mess cleaned and then we'll take you home."

The area wasn't really a mess at all in my opinion. I suppose it was another "woman" thing. She cleared the table, wiped the counter down and we proceeded to the truck. Kayla and I rounded up the dogs, which wasn't much of a chore, since they were still resting on the front porch. We loaded them in the back of the pickup and left for the short drive half way around the mile section to meet Kayla's dad and brother.

The Wilson family homestead area was well maintained, especially when compared to most farms I had seen. The lawn had been recently mowed and the grass along the sidewalk to the house had even been edged. The place was free of eyesores normally associated with a farm. I saw no junk piles or evidence of broken down equipment. Even vegetation around trees, outbuildings and under machinery had been sprayed or manually trimmed. I made a mental note to finish my own weed whacking at the barn and windmill areas, when I returned home.

Our little troupe pulled up to the house just as a slender man of about six feet in height came out to greet us.

"I'd be James Wilson," the middle aged man said. "Matthew told me you had Kayla with you and were coming over. Please stay and visit awhile, won't you? I hope she hasn't been a pest. She likes to go 's'ploring', as she puts it."

"It's just 'cause there's nothin' to do 'round here and me and Jay Jay get bored."

"Kayla, it's 'Jay Jay and I' and you know that."

"Yes sir," she replied and then asked if she could stay outside and show Oro around.

"That girl's English is not what I'd like it to be and here I heard both of you are teachers."

"Well, Lea teaches freshman English and I'm currently on a leave of absence. I really don't know if I will return to teach history next fall or not."

"James," Lea began, "I must say one thing about Kayla. She has not been a pest, whatsoever. I spent a delightful time visiting with her earlier, which was the first time we had actually met."

"Yes," I broke in, "it was and she's really a cool kid. While she was having a snack with Lea, Jay Jay and Oro had a great time chasing each other in the yard. Oro really does need another big dog around to play with. Kayla and Jay Jay are welcome at Rainbow Acres any time, as long as it's OK with you."

Lea jumped in with, "Here's a thought ... why don't you and the kids come over on this Saturday, around noon, for a cookout? Will is always looking for an excuse to fire up the grill."

"That's nice of you to ask, Lea. It would be a good time to get to know each other. Neighbors are, as you've noticed, a little few and far between out here."

Lea and I chatted with James for a period of time over iced tea and Little Debbie treats, before we left for home. We were all gathered around the Dodge Ram when Matt, aka Matthew, depending upon who was talking to him, came walking up from the barn. It appeared that he would walk right past us without a word, but James stopped him.

"Matthew, make no plans for this Saturday afternoon. We are going for a picnic over at Will and Lea's place."

Lea walked towards the boy and held out her hand to shake.

"I've seen you at school, haven't I? Aren't you in Mr. Arnold's English class?"

Matt simply nodded his head in affirmation. To his pleasure, I'm sure, we only remained for a few more minutes before he was released from the ordeal of having to meet company.

On our return trip, Lea brought up the subject of the boy.

"Will, did you notice that Matt acted a little peculiar?"

"He certainly wasn't outwardly sociable. Maybe he needed to go to the bathroom. I get antsy when I have to go and get held up for any reason. Oro, did you pick up on anything to explain his actions?"

"Nothing in particular, but he was definitely agitated. His thoughts were primarily about how he didn't have time for 'chit, chat,' as he put it."

I relayed Oro's answer to Lea.

"Oh, well, I'm sure it was nothing personal."

CHAPTER 12

THE COOKOUT

MY MORNING ROUTINE began normally, with a cup of Folgers (Today I chose my favorite, a French vanilla flavor) and a once over of *The Wichita Eagle's* front page. I then looked for stories from a few of their staff writers, who I knew.

I settled down to read Barbara Baker's words of wit. She was my guide a few months ago, in a fun filled, but informative, tour of the paper's facilities. Since that meeting, I've been working to expand the scope of my column, through self-syndication, but have had no success yet, of getting it placed in *The Eagle.*

My mind soon wandered and took in the neat condition of the area around the Wilson home. Following our visit to their farm a few days earlier, I had worked to clean up around the barn, windmill and other places where landscaping had been partially neglected.

Since I wasn't working full time on anything in particular, I set myself a goal to be more critical of how Rainbow Acres looked. Just because I was wealthy beyond most people's imagination was no reason for me to become lazy and nonproductive.

Even though the appearance of the grounds today was certain to pass Lea's inspection, I thought I'd take a walk around to make sure. Oro must have been monitoring my thoughts.

"Will, quit worrying so much. The place looks great. By the way, while you have the paper in hand, will you read 'Charlie Brown' to me?"

"Oro, I thought you were napping?"

"I was, but you were so deep in thought, you woke me."

"You're right and I'm sorry."

I would, however, have to postpone my self-proclaimed chore and reading the funnies to Oro, for Lea quietly entered the kitchen. Oro's tail began to thump, thump, thump on the floor, which was his usual way of greeting anyone, while in the prone position. Little else moved except for his eyes, as they followed her across the room to the fridge, where she withdrew a bottle of orange juice.

She greeted us. "Good morning, boys and what are you sorry about, Will?"

"Hello, Doe. Oh, I was thinking so hard about what I wanted to do today, that my thoughts woke Oro. I thought you'd be sleeping in on your day off. If I woke you up too, I'm sorry for a second time already on this new day. I tried not to make any unnecessary noise."

"Relax, Dear. You didn't wake me, but it's well past seven, which is sleeping in for me. I hope your heavy thinking included preparing for our picnic later?"

"Yes, in fact I was making mental notes of things to do to get the place in tiptop shape for our visitors."

"I think the place looks fine, Dear and I'm sure the little party will be fun. I think you and James could become good friends. It will give us a chance to know Matt better and Kayla's already a fun kid to have around."

"I agree, Doe. Well, I must get with it ... right after I read some of the funnies to Oro."

I kept myself busy with the weed eater on detail work at various areas around the home and outbuildings. I also decided to mow and do some tree trimming that I had neglected along the trail that went to the back of the property and around the pond.

I lost track of time when I began picking up litter that

had blown, from who knows where, into the shelterbelt; a mixture of evergreen and deciduous trees and shrubs that were frequently planted around homes in the country. Several rows of thick cover, like pines, cedars and junipers were planted on the north, to help break the cold winds in the winter.

Deciduous trees and shrubs were planted to the south, to block hot summer winds. Since those trees lose their leaves in the winter, the sun's rays aren't block, which helped to warm the home and area enclosed by the shelterbelt during periods of cold weather. OK, enough with the trivia lesson about what a shelterbelt is. Let's get back to business.

As usual, Lea had planned everything in great detail and by her schedule, I was running behind. When morning managed to work its way towards noon, I began setting up the grill for our little cookout party. As an excuse for my tardiness, the winds had picked up from the south and I was forced to move the cooking operations to the north side of the house.

A truly portable grill is a benefit and almost a necessity in Kansas. It's said that if you don't like the weather here, just wait a few minutes, because it will soon change. OK, I know the saying is pretty lame and it's not just said in Kansas, because I've heard the words repeated in other areas of the country. I suppose no one knows who deserves the original credit for the expression.

"Will, I see Kayla and Jay Jay coming across the field. They are almost to the row of evergreens in the shelterbelt."

I looked around in the direction of Oro's gaze and saw the girl and her dog. They were just entering the outside edge of the windbreak. I called out to her and waved.

"Yo', Kayla, we're over here on the porch."

Oro had already left me and was in a dead run towards

the pair to greet his new friend and Kayla. The girl soon made it to the porch after dodging the rough and tumble play of the dogs.

"Hi, Mr. Jacobs. We decided to take a hike this way across the field, instead of waiting for the others. They will be coming over in the truck. Me and Jay Jay were ready for a long time and dad said if I couldn't calm down and wait for them, then we could just walk over here. So we did."

"That's fine Kayla and I know Oro is elated to have Jay Jay here early. I get a little impatient myself, at times, so I know how you must have felt."

"Yes, that's how I was. In-pay-shunt is a fifth grade word. I know what it means, but I don't know how to spell it."

"Well, you'll learn that pretty soon, so be patient." Kayla caught on to the jest with a smile and I continued. "Say, I still need to clean the grill. Why don't you go inside and visit with Lea and see if she'd like you to bring anything outside."

"Good, I like to help. I'll be right back."

She had not been gone long when a one-ton, diesel truck came up the driveway and stopped by the porch. James Wilson got out from behind the wheel and was followed by Matt. He was riding in the truck bed and jumped over the side to join his dad. They walked around the front of the truck and approached the steps.

"I see Jay Jay made it over, so I'll assume Kayla is here too," James said after thanking me for inviting them over.

"Yes, she's inside where Lea has probably put her to work," I responded. "Let's go in and get this party rolling."

We all entered, except for the dogs, who were playing tug-a-war with a four-foot section of large diameter rope. James uttered a few "ohs" and "ahs" upon entering. The awesomeness of the house had that affect on virtually everyone who stepped through its doors. Actually, I often feel that way when I enter the house through the front.

We walked through the entry way and the main room,

that we (mostly Lea) called "the gathering place," to reach the kitchen; where we found Lea. Once the formalities had concluded, Lea offered a grand tour of the house, which she always enjoyed doing. I could have conducted the walk through, but I generally allowed Lea the privilege of showing off the place. Besides, I had work to do, which Lea casually reminded me.

"Matt, if you don't care about the twenty-five-cent tour, you could help me."

The boy didn't reply verbally, but didn't hesitate to follow me out through the kitchen, pantry and mudroom to the back yard.

"Thank you for getting me out of girl stuff, Mr. Jacobs."

"I could tell you weren't too thrilled about being shown through the house."

We walked to where the grill was and were met by the dogs.

"Will, you're going to make sure a few hot dogs accidentally make their way to the ground for us, aren't you?"

"Of course."

After a slight pause, Matt asked, "Of course what, Mr. Jacobs?"

"Oh, nothing. I was just talking out loud ... it's a quirk I have."

I had Matt replace the old lava briquettes in the cooker with new ones, while I finished cleaning the grill sections. The dogs opted to lie down near us for a break from horsing around in the yard. I don't know why "dogging around" never took off as a legitimate expression. I saw that Oro remained alert to what Matt and I were doing, but Jay Jay was soon asleep.

Oro responded to my observation. *"He's young and needs his rest."*

"I see." Immediately following my response to Oro's silent comment, I looked over at the boy, who was eyeing me with a peculiar expression on his face. I waved my hand in the air and said with a smile, "Don't mind me

Matthew. At times, I'm in a different world, but don't be afraid; I'm quite harmless."

Within a short time, our preparations were complete. "I believe we are set to light the grill. Since the house tour should be finishing up soon, why don't you go out front and bring the lawn chairs from there around to here. I'll go in and get the meat tray, so we can get this cookout going. I'm already in the dog house a little for being behind on my duties."

Matt left to follow my directions and Oro looked at me with a bigger than usual smile on his face.

"Oro, with the look you're giving me, you've come up with something, so spit it out, big boy."

"I wish to follow up on your thought earlier about 'dogging around.' Why don't people talk about being in the 'horse barn' or something along those lines, instead of being in the 'dog house,' when they are in trouble?"

"Good point," I replied with a laugh. "I don't have an answer, but I've always said that English was a peculiar language."

"It certainly is. On a more professional note … Matthew, I believe, is upset about how his life is going. He wants to go to college this fall after graduating from high school, but his dad says he can't afford the cost. Matthew feels that he wants to keep him at home to work on the farm and be expected to carry on the farming tradition of his forefathers."

"Really? That is interesting."

I was about to enter the mudroom, but the touring party began to exit the house. James was in front with the iced-down cooler of assorted beverages. Kayla followed with a basket filled with napkins and eating utensils and Lea was carrying a foil-covered tray of burgers and dogs in one hand and a plastic sack full of different kinds of chips in the other.

"Kayla," Lea said, "could you be a dear and run back in and get the small ice chest that we put the other fixings in that needed to be kept cold?"

"Oh, I see you've brought out the drinks. James, I'm

sorry if you were expecting a cold beer. I quit drinking a number of years ago and simply don't buy the stuff anymore."

"No sweat, Will. I have a 'cold one' every now and again at home, but a Coke or a Pepsi will do just fine."

"What is the holdup, Will?" Lea said in a gruff voice, while sporting a smile. "We are starving."

"I've just now lit the grill, so it won't be long, Doe."

The afternoon's conversation progressed on the light side and an enjoyable time was had by all, it seemed, including Matt, although he spoke very little. To back up what Oro had said to me earlier, we learned that James was indeed a third generation farmer and expected his son to carry on in his footsteps.

Lea and I were quite surprised to find out a few facts about the history of our property. James' grandfather had owned over 10,000 acres of land, which included the whole section that Rainbow Acres was a part of. The house was, in fact, his Grand Papa's home.

Times were tough during a period of several years, when weather was not being kind to farmers in the Midwest. Winter temperatures had been extremely harsh, and little snow fell for moisture and ground cover. They were followed by drier than average times in the spring, combined with arid summers.

The most senior Wilson was pushing eighty and his health was failing. James and his father could not handle all the farming chores. Because of this and the financial condition of the family, the decision was made to sell the home and half of its section of land. James' grandfather moved to a small place in town and passed away within a year after leaving the farm and his father succumbed to a heart attack only five years after that.

Today had been the first day in twenty years that James

had been in the house, but he remembered what it was like. He complimented us on how we had modernized it, but kept the grandeur and the home's character intact.

The conversation lasted much longer than the meal and would have gone on until dark probably, but James and the kids had evening chores to do and had to leave. The cookout had started what would become a long term friendship between our two families.

CHAPTER 13

FINAL WEDDING PLANS

SLOWLY, BUT SURELY, our rather lengthy "To Do" list for the wedding was reduced in size. This was a good thing, for the event was a mere three days away. Family members from both clans, who didn't live in the immediate vicinity, were beginning to arrive in town. Lea and I made Rainbow Acres available to the out-of-towners, since the home was large.

This was not the case for the church, which was quaint in stature, but small size. Lea had limited wedding invitations to fifty. She painstakingly worked to come up with an adults-only list and hoped that no one's feelings would be hurt for being left off. To balance things somewhat, around three hundred souls had been invited to the reception.

Pat, Lea's mother and Betty, her favorite aunt, were the only temporary boarders, who had accepted the offer to stay with us at the house through the festivities. They arrived a week earlier from Kansas City to assist Lea wherever needed. Since the decision was made to have the reception at our home, it was getting most of the attention at the present time.

I was particularly concerned with keeping abreast of the weather and it looked like Mother Nature was going to cooperate. The first half of the seven-day forecast looked great. It was expected to be sunny and not as hot as a typical July day in Kansas. Even the winds were supposed to be light and variable, another atypical occurrence for those who live in the Midwest. Lea wanted most of the activities to take place outdoors; so normal wind speeds of around fifteen miles per hour with gusts on top of that, would surely hamper most of those plans.

I headed for the kitchen with Oro to see if we could manage an in-between breakfast and lunch snack. We ran into Lea, Pat and Betty in the large dining room. They were hand printing personal nametags for the guests and seating placards for the reception tables that would be rented later.

"I didn't know you were going to the trouble of using fancy clip-on name tags." I had directed my remark to no one in particular, but Lea replied.

"The cheap variety, on a roll, seems to only stick to the roll. They would simply end up being unnecessary lawn litter for you to pick up."

"OK, I see your point. Thanks for thinking of me."

"You're welcome, Dear. Now, what do you need?"

"Lea, I didn't mean to interrupt, but your favorite guys are a tad bit hungry from all the outside yard work we've been doing. I just thought I'd pick up a few cookies and dog treats to recharge our batteries."

"Will, through the window it looked as if you two were only playing throw and fetch with a tennis ball."

"Oh, that ... uh, I should have known to goof off on the other side of the house. At any rate, we really are hungry and I promise we will get down to business and ..."

"All right Dear, quit groveling, get your snacks and vamoose. We are deeply involved in girl talk and what we are going to do Friday night."

"Oh, I almost forgot ... the bachelorette party. Pat, are you and Betty going out to chaperone my bride-to-be? My mother told me she would not be attending some of the planned activities, since she doesn't wish to stay up very late."

"Will," Pat began, "I've spoken to your mother and she will be going out to eat with us girls, too. Then we are taking in a movie afterwards. Lea is not planning anything wild, so you needn't worry about her."

"Hey, you didn't call the women 'guys' like most people do."

Pat began to respond, but Lea broke in with, "Mom, leave it alone. Trust me, you don't want to go there."

I would have been defensive for the verbal snub concerning one of my pet peeves (people calling females "guys"), but I saw her grinning at me as she spoke.

"Will, I expect Laura and her kids any minute now. She's been out helping finalize some details for the reception. After these cards and nametags are done we are going to start decorating. Could you keep Lacy and Lex with you?"

"OK. Oro and I could use help outside."

I pulled out a bag of chips and a large dog treat from the pantry and left with, "OK Doe, we are outa' here."

Once outside, I tossed Oro the biscuit. "Lea's on to us buddy. I guess there will be no more messing around until this yard gets cleaned up."

"Right, boss, what can I do to help?"

"Well, how nice of you to ask. A regular 'ole dog would not be able to assist, but of course you are not your garden-variety hound. It would be a great help if you could patrol the yard where I need to mow and pick up the sticks and limbs you can handle.

"What do you want me to do with the sticks that I find?"

"Take them to the kindling pile beside the campfire area by the barn. That will save me a lot of time and probably a backache from all the bending over I would have had to do. When the kids get here, they can help you."

"Good enough. I'll get started and thanks for the treat. By the way, are you going to have a bachelor's party? I heard you inside talking about Lea's party."

"I decided to pass on anything special, but I did ask Gary and James to meet me for lunch tomorrow and check out the new Gander Mountain store that opened downtown. None of us have been to the place yet and I want to pick up a few things that we could use on the Colorado trip."

"I must admit that I am looking forward to our return trip

to the cool of the mountains. While on the subject, I'd like to thank you in advance for taking me along. It isn't every couple, I'm sure, who would take their dog with them on their honeymoon."

"Oro, no matter where we go, I will never consider leaving you behind if there is a way for you to be with us. You must know you are more than just a dog to both of us?

"Yes, I know and I am glad for that. In fact, I've decided to keep you and Lea around as my owners."

"Thanks for the vote of confidence, Oro. Well, here come our helpers. I see Laura's car coming up the drive. Don't forget … right after the greetings, we need to get busy with the tasks at hand. Then we can play."

"Done deal, boss."

Lacy was first out of the minivan, followed by Lex. The two kids charged over to meet us or I should qualify that to say, meet Oro. They loved playing with him, probably in part, because they had no pets at home.

"Hello Laura, you're right on time, as usual. Lea's inside doing stuff. I saw a pile of decorations, so I have a feeling I know what you will soon be doing."

"Good, I'm sure it will be more fun than work."

"If it's OK with you, I could use the kids to help me outside for awhile."

"Sure, work them as long and as hard as you want. They could use some exercise."

"Great, go right in. Lea and our company were in the dining room when I left." As Laura headed for the house, I began to instruct the kids.

"OK, what I need you two to do is pick up all the sticks and limbs that have fallen into the yard, so I can mow a nice area for the upcoming reception party. I'm concerned with everything north and east of the house to the row of trees that surround that part of the yard."

Lex spoke up. "Mr. D., could I mow too?"

"Well, I don't have a problem with you mowing, but I'll have to get your mother's permission first."

Not long after my visit to the kid's school earlier in the year, as part of Donuts for Dad's Day, Lex had asked if he could call me "Mr. D.," which stood for "Dad". I considered it a very special request and was proud to accept the new title.

"By the way, kids, Oro is going to help you. He will show you where to stack what you pick up from the yard."

Lacy, who was standing with Oro, laughed, "Mr. Jacobs, that's funny. How is Oro going to help us?"

"Why don't you just begin the job and see for yourself."

Oro and the kids were soon diligently working on yard clean up. I went inside to talk to Laura concerning Lex's request to mow. She told me it would be fine as long as I made sure he knew how to operate the rider and if I stayed nearby to supervise. I assured her I would watch him.

Outside, I brought the riding mower from the garage and began cutting the grass on either side of the long drive to the county road. I had previously walked that area and removed limbs. After mowing three round trips on each side of the drive, I rode the mower to the side yard, turned it off and called Lex over to join me.

I gave him brief, but adequate instructions on how to properly operate the machine and turned him loose to mow the areas that had been cleared of sticks. I watched him for a few passes around the yard and then called to Lacy. She was playing with Oro again.

"Lacy, why don't you go in and let Lea and your mom know that we are working very hard and need some cookies and a pitcher of lemonade."

"Oh, that sounds good. Cum-on Oro, let's go get some goodies."

It was a productive and fun time for all of us. The next two days of preparations for the wedding and reception went by in a flash.

Everyone in our house was up and taking care of one thing or another before a few hundred thousand other citizens of Wichita were even out of bed on this special Saturday; the day of our wedding.

My mom, who had driven down the afternoon that I showed Lex how to use the riding mower, was helping Lea, Pat and Betty in some form of an assembly line. They were preparing a peculiar looking concoction for 300 dessert cups, which would be placed on trays and set in the floor freezer.

At nine, Laura, Lex and Lucy arrived. I met them outside and within a few minutes saw Matt's truck coming up the drive. He pulled in behind Laura's van and Kayla jumped out.

Oro ran over to greet her, as he had done with the two other kids, but he stopped short.

"Hey, where's Jay Jay? Couldn't he come over? He's not sick, is he?

Before Oro had an anxiety attack, I told him, via mind talk, to calm down and I would find out what was going on.

"Hi Kayla, thanks for coming over to help out. Where's Jay Jay?"

"Oh, Dad thought that you didn't need him running around and getting in the way. That's why I came with Matt. When any of us leave the house in the truck Jay Jay knows to stay home. If I walked over, he would have followed me."

"Well, he wouldn't be a problem. I'm sure Oro is disappointed that you didn't bring him."

"You could go get him, if you want to, Mr. Jacobs."

"I'll call James to see if Oro can go visit."

I pulled out my cell and entered Kayla's home number. Matt, who was standing nearby, talking with Lex, offered to return to get Jay Jay.

"Thanks, but that won't be necessary. Your father has invited Oro over."

"Then I'll drive him back to our house," Matt countered.

"That's not necessary either." I turned to Oro, who had been patiently taking our talk in. "Oro, you may go see Jay Jay, but be back by noon. You will need a bath and grooming for the reception and Laura has agreed to spruce you up for the party."

Oro, with one of his patented smiles, walked past me and in the direction of the Wilson farm. He quipped on his way by, *"Will, you are going to have them totally bewildered with that one."*

He was right. Matthew, Kayla, Lex and Lacy all stood in silence, but looked at each other and at the departing Oro, as if they didn't understand what they knew they had witnessed. It was all I could do to keep from outwardly laughing, but I explained the situation away, as if it were a commonplace event.

"I've told you all before what a smart dog Oro is. He knows what I mean and always obeys."

CHAPTER 14

DEARLY BELOVED

To A RESIDENT from the city, the parking area at the secluded church in the country had an unusual appearance to it. Yes, the surface was a mixture of grasses growing through gravel instead of being concrete or asphalt, but what looked out of place was the presence of a horse and buggy pulled alongside a stretch limo. "Black," the sleek and glistening steed attached to the cart didn't care, for his only interest was in munching from the bag of oats hung over his head by his master.

The stage was set and the main players were in attendance, so there was no reason to keep the blessed event from being carried out on schedule. I didn't feel there was a need to select ushers, due to the limited space for seating guests, but Elsa and her husband volunteered to take on that role for us. The decision was also made to forgo the normal segregation of the patrons (groom's guests right; bride's guests left), since the list of those invited was not divided equally between our families.

The interior of the church was not as dark as when Lea and I first came across the place. An abundance of lanterns were located around the perimeter of the chapel and strategically placed down each side of the aisle. And on either side of the alter stood high reaching spiral standards that held twenty-one lighted candles apiece. Even though the light provided was adequate, those in attendance still had to briefly pause in the entryway to let their eyes adjust to the darker, inside environment.

I was so pleased that most of Lea's ideas about the

ceremony concurred with my wishes. It was to be, by choice, short, but sweet. We saw no need for the large entourage that was the typical makeup of most wedding parties; something I always thought took away from the primary focus of why folks came ... to see the bride and groom.

We also agreed to dispense with the normal, and at times, lengthy spiel from most ministers. His script would begin with "Dearly beloved" and include "you may kiss your bride," but the middle part was drastically edited.

Lea and I (mostly Lea) wanted to prepare and exchange our own vows. She felt it would form a more personal bond between us. When I grumbled slightly about the task, she quickly countered, "And you call yourself a writer." I, of course, said no more.

The ceremony plans were straightforward and simple, for we were not there to impress anyone, but when Lea came down the aisle, escorted by Earl, her father, I was unequivocally impressed. I recall nothing else from the moment, for my bride-to-be had my full attention. I was stunned by the beauty of the woman, as she glided down the pathway and stood beside me.

I had never experienced such an elevated feeling of awe, brought about by Lea's presence. Her eyes were of an intensity I had never witnessed. The flickering of the flames around us made her facial features appear heavenly and angelic. I felt truly blessed.

I looked out at the friends and family assembled before us (we again broke tradition and faced the audience). All fifty seats available for use were occupied. To the right of my mother and between my two sisters sat Oro.

"Will, just in case all the excitement you are experiencing at this moment causes you to forget your vows, you need not worry. I've memorized them for you."

I remembered (for a change) to respond to him telepathically with, "Oro, you are, without a doubt, a most trusted friend and I do believe I may need your assistance."

"No problem, boss. You can count on me."

Somehow, I was able to recite my promises to Lea without error, however my oratory was not devoid of difficulties, for you see, I cried. The tears, limited as they were, clouded my vision, but not mind. I was honored to have been accepted by Lea to be a part of her life, forever and most proud when I heard the final words from the preacher, "I now present to you ... Lea and Will Jacobs."

After a few moments of photo ops outside, the contingency of vehicles that had kept Black company during the wedding, left for the reception.

At Rainbow Acres, James and Laura had volunteered their services to oversee security duties, if needed, and the checking in of folks who would undoubtedly be arriving before the scheduled start time of the party. Many of those who had not been on the invite list for the wedding were already mingling around the premises as our limo, with the immediate family on board, arrived. (Hey! I don't want to hear any flack about the rented "wheels." I had to splurge a little bit, didn't I?)

The gathering went as well as anyone could expect and the weather was absolutely marvelous for any early July day in Kansas. The forecast, for light winds and cooler than normal temperatures, was thankfully accurate.

Our guest sign-in book at the end of the day sported over three hundred names, which was interesting, for the invitation list accounted for fewer than 300. I didn't know exactly what that fact meant, but I wasn't going to dwell on it.

Earl, on the other hand, thought that Lea and I should sit down, go through the names in the guest book and match them with the invitation list. I hadn't been around Lea's dad much, but this confirmed my idea that he over analyzed everything in life. At this point in time, however, there were other matters I deemed more important.

By the time I managed to convince everyone that the party was over, the sun was low in the western sky. Finally Mr. and Mrs. Jacobs were alone. Even Oro had gone home with Jay Jay for a sleepover.

Chapter 15

The Last Gift

"Will, as much as I'd love to stay in bed longer, I think it's time to start the day off with a good breakfast for my hubby."

"Doe, I can eat breakfast later. Besides, we both deserve to goof off for a while longer, after all the work we've done in the past few days. The reception flat wore me out."

"Why do you say that? I thought we had more than ample help to put it all together."

"Yes, we did, but it's more about being mentally exhausted rather than physically. I'm not great at smiling for hours on end, which social functions of any sort require. I also became quite bored with listening to so many of the family suck up to me about this or that. I can't count how often I was pulled aside to hear a story of woe by one relative after another. Money was the issue in each case. We should have handed everyone a loan application when they came onto the property."

"Your frustration is not lost on me, Dear. I noticed that a few of my family even looked at me differently. I suppose it's one of the disadvantages of being rich."

"Exactly, but it certainly beats the alternative ... peace, quiet and poverty."

"I'm going downstairs to fix my guy a big breakfast, so you need to get up and do whatever you do in the morning. It will be ready within the half hour. Oh, by the way, don't forget to make the bed."

"Oh no, Doe. Is the honeymoon over already?"

Lea donned her robe and flashed me a lovely smile, as she left the bedroom and headed for the stairs. Before leaving she added, "And my new saying will be, 'just get 'er done,' so what do you think?"

"I went to bed with an angel and woke up with a nanny. Oro won't believe it."

I lay there for a few more minutes, then got up, slipped my robe on and ... made the bed. Once downstairs, I entered the kitchen, pulled out a chair and watched the woman of my dreams prepare the meal.

I thought about walking down the drive to retrieve the paper, but my attention was diverted towards the mudroom. A head stuck through the dog door with a rolled newspaper in its mouth.

"Oro, you read my mind. What a good boy. Doe, Oro's here."

Lea didn't turn around from her cooking duties, but greeted him with, "Oro, did you have a fun sleepover at Jay Jay's house last night?"

He did not "speak" at first, but entered the kitchen and placed the paper in my hand.

"Yes, I did, and thanks for asking, Lea."

I started to repeat his remark to her, but was a little startled when she whirled around and looked at us with a very peculiar expression on her face.

"Will?" came out of her mouth, but nothing else, as she stared at Oro.

"What is it, Doe?" I said.

"Oro, did I just hear you or am I dreaming?"

Now, I was the one who must have had the peculiar facial expression.

"Lea, you aren't dreaming, so the answer is yes, you heard me."

"How did you ..."

"I didn't do anything. Somehow it just happened, but since I gave neither of you presents yesterday, I'll take credit for it being a belated wedding gift to you, Lea."

"Oh, my, this could very well be the greatest gift I have ever received. I'm absolutely speechless."

In actuality, it was me who was speechless. I just gazed at the two of them, as Lea bent down and gave Oro an enduring hug. I finally understood what had taken place here.

"This is awesome news, Oro. When did you discover that she was in the zone, or whatever it was?"

"Well, let's see … I had picked up the paper for you and was just sitting on the back porch waiting for you to come out. I didn't want to interrupt you, ya' know."

I started to say that he wouldn't have been interrupting us, but Lea put her hand to my mouth to stop me from speaking.

"Continue, Oro," she said.

Oro smiled and went on with, *"I was thinking about one of the songs that the DJ played at the reception yesterday, when you thought,"* as he looked at Lea, *"'why is Will humming that song. I thought he didn't like music.'"*

I pulled a chair out for Lea and was allowed to speak.

"You'd better sit down, Doe. You look a little glazed over, like you might faint on us or come down with some other medical problem."

She sat down and a huge tear rolled out from one eye and made its way down her cheek.

"I can't explain how incredibly happy I am. In the last two days, two fantastic events have occurred in my life …" She paused and then finished, saying, "I feel truly blessed."

"Ironically enough, Lea, I spoke those very words yesterday; right before we exchanged our vows."

Oro decided to lighten up the mood and added, *"You'd better hold on, Lea, since good things are said to come in threes, there's no telling what may happen next."*

"You have been reading my book, haven't you, boy?"

We were all about to laugh, but the smell of smoke from over fried bacon suddenly hit us at the same time.

"Oops," one or all of us said, just as the smoke alarm went off. The news from Oro had been so phenomenal that nothing else mattered.

I silenced the alarm while Lea hit the exhaust fan switch and Oro laughed at how quickly we were jumping around. For the rest of the day it seemed like none of us could keep a smile off our mugs.

CHAPTER 16

TO YOUR MARKS ... GET SET

D EAR, I'M GOING to Wal-Mart to take care of most of the
shopping list for our trip and Laura's due to arrive
soon. What are your plans?"

"Yes, Mrs. Jacobs, I know. I'm also expecting Matt and
Kayla. The girls can help Laura and the boys will help me
getting the Eagle washed and ready to go. When you return,
pull over to it and unload whatever can be stored now."

"All right, Mr. Jacobs. That's a good task to complete
today. On my list are a few supplies for her, but I believe
she has enough of everything to clean today."

"OK, so we'll see ya' later, Love."

Oro and I decided to sit around and bond while waiting
for the two mini-groups of helpers to arrive.

I had already enlisted the aid of Matt to take care of
many jobs around the place, while we were away. I knew
how tiresome some tasks often become when one works
alone. I had frequently observed Lex's attitude and
actions while he was here and concluded that he would
be a capable helper.

With that in mind, I had asked Matt if he would like
to have Lex's assistance while we were gone. He seemed
pleased with the proposition, so I planned to follow through
with the next step of the hiring process and ask Lex if he
were interested in working with Matt.

*"Will, I believe you are making a nice move in putting
Laura's kids on the payroll, so to speak. I know they have
helped a lot with chores and not asked for anything in return
from their mother. Including Kayla is good, too."*

"Oro, you have been eavesdropping again, haven't you?"

"Hey, boss, it's not my fault. You shouldn't think so hard."

"Yeah, you're right, my friend. It's nice, in a way, how you usually save me time in asking for your opinion, because you already know what's on my mind. And here come two of our little helpers now."

We made our way down the walk to the drive and met Laura and her brood.

"Hello kids. Go play with Oro, while I speak with your mom for a bit."

I saw they each had brought a tennis ball and it took no coaxing for them to comply with my request.

"Good morning, Will," Laura said and anxiously continued with, "is there something wrong?"

"No, everything's fine. I just wanted to ask if you might like to have Kayla come over to help you while we are on our trip. I would take care of paying her something for being here."

"I don't really need her, but it is nice having her around to keep Lacy company, when she's not helping me."

"OK, I can understand that. What I'd like to do is give each of the girls at least five bucks for the time they are here with you. I know both of them have often helped Lea and me with this or that and their presence has been fun for Oro, too. I'll let you decide the size of the gratuity. Will that plan be OK with you?"

"Yes sir."

"Good. On another note, I'd like to ask Lex if he'd be interested in working with Matt while we are gone and I would pay him a few bucks an hour when he helps out. Would that be OK with you, too?

"Will, that would be very nice of you to do that. I'm sure Lex would be thrilled."

"Good, I'll ask him and you can make the deal with Lacy. By the way, if you ever need Matt to help with anything, like heavy work, feel free to ask. I've already told him to let you know that he is available."

"Thank you, Will. I'll keep that in mind."

I put a halt to the fetching game between Oro, Lex and Lacy. I told Lex that I needed him and told Lacy to go speak with her mom. I presented the boy the offer to work with Matt and help his mom, whenever needed. His eyes really lit up when I mentioned that I would give him ten dollars each day that he helped, while they were at Rainbow Acres.

He was quite excited about the prospect of having, as he put it, "A real job, for real money."

I went inside to relay the outcome of my talk with Lex to Laura. Lacy ran up and gave me an enormous hug.

Rapidly she threw out, "Thank you sooooo much for giving me and Kayla money. I don't know what she will do with her money, but I'm gonna save some of mine for college, so mom won't have to work so hard to send me to college and ..."

"Hold on girl," Laura interrupted. "You need to slow down and calm down."

"I know mama, but it's really exciting, don't you think?"

"Yes, Dear, it is exciting. Now why don't you get Oro's big brush from the back and groom him for Will."

"Okay, Mom." She started to leave, but added, "Thanks again, Mr. Jacobs. You're sooooo nice and we love you."

"You are very welcome, Lacy," I said as she took off down the hallway towards the mudroom, where we kept Oro's things.

"Laura, I take it she agreed to the offer?"

"Nothing gets past you, does it, Mr. J.," she said with a grin.

"Nope, I'm not too quick on my feet anymore, but I've still got it upstairs. I don't know if you've seen it or not, but your kids and James' two really pair up nicely. The two boys act like brothers and any outsider would think that Kayla and Lacy are sisters."

"Yes, I've been aware of that early on, right after I began to work for you. I was wondering if any of the children have told you any little tales about James and me?"

"No, no they haven't. Don't tell me the 'ole senses are failing me. What might they have told me?"

"Well, James and I have been going out, on occasion. I can hardly believe that between the four of them, you haven't heard anything."

"Not a peep, but the news is nice to hear. I'm not much of a matchmaker, but I can see how you two would make a good couple. I'm surprised Oro never clued me in."

"What?" she said, with a puzzled look on her face.

"Ahhhh, well ... as much time as he spends with all the kids, you'd think he'd tell me, wouldn't you?"

"Yeah, right," Laura said with a laugh. "Mr. Jacobs, I had better quit goofing off and get back to work, unless there's something else you'd like to talk to me about?"

"No, that's about it for now. I guess we will be gone before your next scheduled visit, so Lea and I will leave you any notes on the kitchen counter, along with our immediate itinerary and emergency contact numbers. Oh, I almost forgot ... here's a set of keys, too."

I left Laura and went in search of Oro. I had already gotten so used to the idea that he could communicate with Lea that it seemed only natural to me that he could "talk" to anyone. I was pretty sure Laura simply thought I was playing around. I found him lying down on the front porch, panting.

"Hello, Will," he managed with an effort.

I sat down beside him on the top step. "Hey, fella, what's the matter?"

"I'm exhausted! Those two don't realize that it's a lot easier to throw the ball around than it is to fetch it and bring it back. Here, hide these," he told me, as he pulled two tennis balls out from under his chest with his teeth.

I had to choke back a laugh. "OK and I'll tell them not to run you so much. Say, what do you know about Laura and James going out on dates?"

"Nothing, but Lacy told Lex to find out what Matt thought about their mom."

"I see. Well, maybe there's no big romance going on between the two."

"If there is, they are keeping it pretty quiet."

After a few minutes, Oro was able to breathe normally and the stillness of the late morning was broken by the distinct clicking sound from Matt's near antique pickup coming up the drive.

"Good deal, they are right on time. I'm going to have the boys give the Eagle a good pre-trip cleaning. Oro, go find Lex and get him to follow you back to the shed."

"Like Lassie does?"

"When have you seen Lassie?"

"I've seen reruns of the old TV show. I've heard you say that I'm many times better than Lassie ever thought of being, so I thought I'd investigate to see who Lassie was."

"It's true; now prove it and find Lex."

We had three TV's in the house and it wasn't unusual to find Oro watching one of them. His favorites involved almost any program with animals … imagine that.

I met Matt, who had brought Kayla along with him. After a few moments of "what's up" talk, I sent Kayla into the house to work with Laura and Lacy.

"By the way, Matt. Your truck is sounding sicker than usual. Why don't you take it into Doug's Auto in Haysville, and have them look it over. You can have Doug bill me for the work. I want you to have reliable transportation while we're gone."

"That's really decent of you, Mr. Jacobs. I can take it in later today."

Lex soon showed up with Oro and I instructed my newly hired young men on how to properly wash the motor home.

Weather predictions for the days after the wedding looked like normal summer conditions would be returning to the Wichita area. Since temperatures were due to climb into the high 90's, mixed in with an elevated humidity, we (mostly I) had made the decision to drive overnight on our much anticipated journey to Colorado.

Lea had reservations about the plan and felt that driving all night was not a safe idea. "You are the one who will be doing all of the driving, Will and I can not stay awake throughout the night to keep you company."

"Doe, I plan to have all the tasks on the list we prepared earlier completed by noon or thereabouts. After that, I will take a long nap and be good to go. Traveling at night, when the temperature is cooler, will be easier on the Eagle, too."

Oro offered his assistance. *"If I could help in any way, please let me know. Lea, if you want to sleep through most of the overnight part of the trip, I'd be more than happy to pester Will to keep him awake and alert."*

"You certainly could help him with that, Oro and thank you for volunteering to give up your sleep. I would be a zombie if I tried to stay awake all night."

"That's no problem … I can always catch up with a few dog naps when we pull in for fuel or food."

"I've only heard of a 'cat nap,' but I guess cats shouldn't have exclusive rights to coin the phrase," Lea quipped.

"Seriously, Lea," I chipped in, "it will be fine and completing the initial travel during the night would be like having an extra day for our trip, since we wouldn't be burning daylight hours on the road."

"All right, boys, I give in. I do have some great traveling music on discs that you may choose from to help keep you awake."

"You can bring them along for your pleasure, Lea, but I checked out two books on tape from the library."

"Will told me about them earlier. They sound like they will be quite entertaining."

"I had not thought of that option. What titles did you check out?"

"Two classics … Agatha Christy's <u>Thirteen at Dinner</u> and J. Conan Doyal's, <u>The Hound of the Baskervilles</u>."

"Those should be interesting enough to keep your mind active while driving. I only hope I don't get involved with listening to them. I'm a longtime Christy fan myself."

"OK, I won't play the tapes until after you have turned in."

It was settled. We would make the first leg of the trip through the night. And so it was … on the day before my annual pilgrimage, of sorts, to Colorado.

CHAPTER 17

Go!

MURPHY, OF MURPHY'S Law fame, must have been on vacation, because nothing of a negative nature occurred to delay our trip's scheduled departure time. Our little party was on the road shortly after the late evening news aired. This would put us in Pueblo for an early morning breakfast at an east side McDonalds, where I am a regular. I didn't say I was a frequent customer, but stopping there once each year should technically qualify me as being a regular.

By eleven, Lea remarked sluggishly, "I woke up too early this morning, Dear and went without a nap, so I need some sleep. Feel free to wake me if you want me to bring you anything. Oro, are you ready to take over for me?"

"Be glad to Lea. Does that mean that I can sit in your seat? Then I'll be able to look out over the dash and see the road?"

"I have no problem with that and I'm sure Will doesn't either, do you Dear?"

"No, but let's put a sheet or large towel over the seat so Lea doesn't pick up your hair on her clothes. No disrespect intended, Oro."

"I understand, Will."

"Boys, as we begin this trip together, I feel we are more of a family now that I have the ability to communicate with you directly, Oro, as you have been able to with Will."

"I know we are all pleased with that occurrence and I swear I haven't a clue to explain what happened that allows us to be on the same wavelength or whatever it may be."

"I will have to admit that I have often felt left out ... like not being a full partner in the family, if you know what I mean. But don't get me wrong. I'm not saying either of you made me feel uncomfortable ..."

I interrupted with, "Lea, Oro and I couldn't be happier about the new development and ..."

Now it was Oro's turn to break in. *"Lea, I could sense that you were, at times, put off a little when you weren't always a direct part of the talk between Will and me. I was sad that I could do nothing about it and believe me I tried to make it happen. Those days are thankfully over."*

"Well, the breakthrough will free up a lot of my time, because I won't have to always be Mr. In-between Guy anymore."

"True," said Lea, "and I shall be able to catch Oro's true wit first hand. I'm sure some of his humor was lost through exchanges in the past ... not to imply that you were a poor interpreter, Dear."

"Oh, I'd be the first one to admit my inadequacies in the task."

"Yes, Lea," Oro brought out with a smile, *"you will be able to obtain information straight from the horse's mouth ... so to speak."*

"Will, if I were a betting person, I might place a wager that Oro has been reading your <u>Grizzly's This 'N That</u> book. I know the 'horse's mouth' saying is included in it somewhere."

Before I could respond, Oro did. *"Actually, I have and with more practice, I've become a much better page turner, too."*

We all had a good laugh on that one. Lea threw a sheet over her seat and retreated to the middle of the rig to take a snooze on the couch. Oro jumped into the vacated captain's chair, as I slid the first cassette of the Christy audio book into the player on the dash.

"I'll wait awhile before starting the tape, Oro. That will give Lea enough time to fall asleep."

I set the cruise control on the Eagle at 65 and the night

engulfed us as we left the lights of the city behind. We were soon gliding across the plains of western Kansas towards Colorado.

The previous year, I had stopped frequently for fuel, which was not a necessity, due to the rig's large capacity fuel tank. The stops were to break up the trip some and to sightsee or shop; for Lea's benefit. Since we were traveling overnight on this trip, there was no need to stop for the previous reasons, but I had made plans to make pit stops in Dodge City and Lamar, Colorado, for Oro.

Lea woke when we made the stops and each time took a brief walk with Oro and me, but returned, with apologies, to the couch to resume her beauty rest. It was OK with me, for I had no difficulty staying awake with Oro's company and the story tapes.

We rolled through Fowler, CO, at a little past six a.m. The light from a new day's sunrise was slowly consuming the darkness. The silhouettes of the Front Range mountains and prominent peaks were soon visible.

"Oro, would you rouse Lea from her slumber? She wanted to be awake when the mountains first came into view."

He left his spot, without any mental exchange, and went towards the couch in back. I glanced around to see his nose slowly wedge itself under Lea's chin. Lea reclaimed her seat from Oro and took in the view before us.

When we arrived on the fringes of Pueblo, we pulled into a gas station with "my" McDonald's nearby. We would take a break to feed the Eagle and its passengers. The cost of filling the "tanks" of the crew was quite meager when compared to the fuel bill of the motor coach.

Within a couple of hours, we passed through Canon City, near the Royal Gorge and then Salida. We drove on without stopping until we pulled into the gift shop area at the top of Monarch Pass. The successful completion of the mile climb to 11,300 feet warranted a rest break for the Eagle.

I took Oro for a walk into the wooded area near the parking lot, while Lea went in to browse. After our stroll, I took a seat on steps leading up to a cable car that provided rides to the top of this part of the Continental Divide.

"How are you holding up, Will?"

"I'm doing fine. Sunrise and the fresh coffee back in Pueblo helped, but being back in the majestic mountains has rejuvenated my spirits. I've missed them so."

"I can fully understand your feelings. It's like a different world here, when compared to back home."

As Oro finished his comment, Lea exited the shop and walked to us. She carried no sacks, which surprised me, but held out an ice cream cone to me.

"Thank you, Doe."

"You are welcome, Dear. I also have an ice cream sandwich for Oro."

"Wow! How did you know I wanted ice cream?"

"Oro, did you forget that I'm able to pick up on your thoughts now. I 'heard' that you wanted some just after we pulled into the parking lot."

"I saw the ice cream advertisement on the shop's marquee. I must have strongly pondered the idea."

"Lea, I thought you'd like to take the gondola ride to the peak? There's quite a good view of the whole area at the top."

"That sounds like fun. Can we take Oro with us?"

"I don't see any reason why he couldn't come along. You'd better grab your coat, because it's sure to be much cooler at the top."

After Lea returned from the Eagle with a jacket, we proceeded up the steps to the ride, paid the fee and the three of us were shortly on our way. The lift operator only asked that we keep Oro on his leash.

The ride to the top took only a few minutes and involved an elevation gain of about 1,000 feet. When I was in better shape and climbed 14er's each summer it would have taken me an hour to accomplish that distance.

Once at the top, the car stopped and we stepped onto a platform that led up to a circular observation deck with a mounted binocular at each of the four nautical directions.

"Will, this is absolutely an awesome view. Thank you for mentioning it. Why didn't we do this last year? I remember we crossed over the pass on the way home."

"Yes, we did, but it was overcast."

"Oh, I see. Oro, what do you think of the view."

"It is quite impressive. By the way, did you see the size of the marmot that just went behind those boulders over there?"

"No, I didn't and don't ask me to let you off the leash, so you can chase it. Remember what the attendant said?"

"Yes I know. I just thought I'd give it a shot. Are we, while I've got critters on the brain, going to Rainbow Lake again, where I can chase Fluffy and his friends?"

"Oro, I'm sure Will will be taking us to the lake. There goes those two 'wills' again. Dear, if I don't call you 'Dear' or another term of endearment, I will call you 'Grizzly.'"

"That works for me, Doe, since I'm quite fond of my nickname."

"Now back to your question, Oro. I don't need to read Will's mind to know that Rainbow Lake may be his favorite spot in Colorado."

"Yes, Lea, that's true, but I believe you enjoy the place too."

"I do love the area and it will always be special to me, because that is where I first found out about your gift, Oro."

We completed our scenic mountaintop visit and rest break at Monarch Pass and now faced the slow task of negotiating the turns of the route's descent. The always-present warning signs for truckers to stay in low gear were prominently posted on the downward side of the mountains. Drivers of other large vehicles, as in our case, needed to heed the advice as well. The speed and forward momentum generated by going downhill can easily end up in the dangerous situation of losing control when unable to slow down to make a turn. In my travels through the mountains, I've seen all sorts of vehicles buried in the deep sand of the emergency pull off ramps.

The Eagle negotiated the route admirably and we pressed on towards Gunnison. We arrived on the east edge of town where I pulled into another one of "my" McDonalds.

"Oro, would you like to take a walk before or after I order the usual for you?"

"I can wait for the walk; let's eat first."

"Do you mean to tell me that you two eat at McDonalds often enough back home that you know what to order?"

"Well, don't forget that we had to fend for ourselves for quite some time before you moved in and began, thankfully I might add, to prepare most of our meals."

"All right, I guess you talked your way out of that one."

"Whew, good thinking, Will. For the record, Lea, we don't go out that often, but I always order the same thing when we do visit McDonalds."

I drove a short distance west to the city park with our "to go" meals, where we took our time to enjoy the food and company in the cool of the late morning, while the Western University marching band provided the entertainment. The field between McDonalds and the park was the college's practice field.

"Now we need to visit Wal-Mart. Lea, I trust you have the shopping list for food and other perishable items that we didn't pick up at home?"

"Yes, Grizzly, Dear. You did remember that the Wal-Mart here is not a super store like all those back in Wichita, so we will have to visit one of the markets to buy groceries."

"Oh, I did forget that and I don't know why they don't have one here yet."

We accomplished the task of purchasing the various items on the food list from Safeway and were soon on the road again to complete the last thirteen miles of our 500-mile journey.

Oro acknowledged our arrival at the site with, *"The Eagle has landed."*

Check-in at Blue Mesa Ranch took only a few minutes, before we were allowed to proceed to our reserved spot on the northwest side of the resort.

The rest of the day was filled with short-term tasks and well-deserved naps. I believe I had one after each campground chore was accomplished. For example: I unhooked the Jeep from the Eagle and took a nap. I stabilized and leveled our classic home on wheels and took a nap. I ate some delicious sandwiches Lea had fixed for a late lunch snack and took a nap. I was, however, able to set up the outside grill, help cook a late evening meal and eat much of it before I traded the naps in for a full-fledged night of sleep. Before retiring, a thought occurred to me.

"Lea, guess what? This is the first night for us to sleep in the Eagle and be in the same bed."

"I hadn't thought of it, but you are right. Sleep well, Dear ... I love you."

"Thank you, Mrs. Jacobs. I love you too."

"Hey, what about me?" came from the hallway outside the door.

"We love you too, Oro," Lea and I said in unison.

"Ditto," he responded.

Chapter 18

Stop and Smell the Flowers

A FTER THE THIRD day of our stay at Blue Mesa Ranch, I felt like I should be doing something more energetic than sitting in the hot tub at the Adult Center, shooting pool at the Recreation Center, playing bingo at the Lodge or sitting in the hot tub.

Oh, I'm not saying I wasn't doing anything that required exercise, because I was. I was undefeated versus Lea in several games of tossing horseshoes and putting around on the miniature golf course at the Sports Complex and did I mention the part about sitting in the hot tub ... as a medicinal and therapeutic treatment for the body?

Actually, my decision to plan an activity away from the confines of the ranch facilities was to appease my companions, who were about to mutiny and leave me to sit in the hot tub by myself.

I heard grumblings first from Lea. "Will, you should be thoroughly rested from doing without sleep for one night and certainly acclimated to the altitude by now, so let's go somewhere."

"OK, Doe, where would you like to go?"

Then my faithful sidekick, Oro, was heard from. *"You said we would be going to Rainbow Lake. Why can't we begin there and then go for a road trip somewhere in the Jeep."*

"OK, you two don't have to gang up on me. We can pack a lunch and leave for the lake within the hour."

So we did. I don't know why I had put off, until now, the drive to Rainbow Lake, which was a trip of less than an hour. It was, as Lea had mentioned before, one of my favorite spots in Colorado. The peace and quiet I found during my visits to the lake would surely be equaled in a countless number of other places around any forest area of the Rockies, but that particular one square mile of Mother Earth's world was special to me for some unexplainable reason.

Oro excused himself as soon as the Jeep came to a stop, in order to chase "Fluffy", his name for any squirrel, whether it lived in Colorado or back home in Kansas. If he were to actually catch one, I do believe he would apologize to the animal for the incident and free him or her, unharmed. The same scenario would probably hold true for rabbits or any other forms of wildlife.

Lea and I casually took a stroll around the crystal clear lake. A narrow trail on the sun exposed part of the landscape meandered through a meadow saturated in fragrances of one sort or another from numerous varieties of wild flowers that boasted an array of colors. An artist would have stopped to capture the beauty of the scene on canvas. We stopped just to take in the serenity of the spot and listen to the hum of the plethora of bees present. We sat, side by side, on a large boulder and said nothing. Before moving on, we (mostly Lea) took pictures of the surroundings, even though we knew the photos would not reproduce the aura of the place.

Once back at the Jeep, Lea brought out a basket of goodies for a mid-afternoon lunch or as I liked to call it, "lupper," similar to brunch being a late morning ... oh, you get it, I'm sure. While in a thinking mood, brought about by Rainbow Lake's influence on me, I spoke to my companions.

"Hey, what would you two think about heading out in the Jeep for a weeklong tour of southwestern Colorado? We could go incognito and camp out."

"It seems to me that I brought up that very same idea a couple of hours earlier. I don't know why I have this gift of

communication with you, Will, if you aren't going to use it, so to repeat myself … I'm up for a road trip."

"Sorry, Oro, I must have been out of the zone."

"Dear, where does the incognito part come into play?"

"Well, who would believe a family of millionaires would be roughing it in a tent."

"It's not that I'm opposed to sleeping in a tent, on occasion, but why would **you** want to … especially for a week?"

"Lea, maybe the altitude gain has affected his logic. I'm sure he will come to his senses later tonight, after he visits the hot tub near our camp site … the one with the motor home sitting on it in place of a tent."

"Oro, do you mean to say that you don't care to sleep out in a tent for a few days? You were doing just that, when I met you last summer."

"That's true, I admit, but it's because Darcie didn't have a Fleetwood Eagle to sleep in."

"Good point, Oro. Dear, if you want to leave the comforts of the Eagle and temporarily become nomadic and wander around, I shall face the challenge with you, even though we specifically left out the part about 'the wife shall serve and obey her spouse' in our vows."

"Count me in, too, as if I had a choice in the matter."

"OK, now we're talking and you aren't fooling me, Oro. I see you trying to fight back that grin of yours. We have ten days before our Chamber of Commerce dinner for Oro at Lake City. We need only to decide on where we stay over and for how long. We have a few days to formulate a plan and make a few reservations before heading west."

The next day Lea and I sat in our comfortable patio chairs under the pulled out awning of the Eagle, while Oro lay in the sun nearby. I was going through the informational AAA Tour Book for Colorado that listed things to do and places to visit in the state. The excellent resource books on travel in every state are available, free, with a Triple A membership.

"Will, I know I want to go to Ouray [you-ray] and spend time at the hot springs in the late evening like we did before."

"OK, that can be arranged. We stayed at the KOA north of town last year. This time we could stay at the National Forest Campground up the mountain side on the south end of town. I hope LaPappion's Bakery is still open, so we (mostly I) can partake in their 'to die for' cinnamon rolls while we're in town. They are almost as good as yours, Love."

"You're lucky you modified that statement, big guy, but I'd have to agree that they have a great dough recipe, which makes a big difference. I wonder if the Alpine Inn near the bakery has sold. I believe you were tempted to buy it last summer."

"I was, but I hadn't totally given up the idea of going back to teach. Thanks to Oro, I believe we (mostly he) can make a big difference in people's lives and I could leave the teaching to younger guys and gals."

"Will, you don't have to give me that much credit for what we can achieve. By myself, I can do nothing."

"How, true you are, my good friend. I feel more important already. OK, let's get back down to business. After Ouray, we'll stay at the camp ground north of Durango, where we crossed paths with Darcie and Oro."

"We can reminisce our time spent there. Do you think that same squirrel, Fluffy, will be there?"

"I don't know, Oro, but I hope we don't reenact the stolen car scene for the sake of our personal safety."

"Yes, Dear, that was an experience a little bit on the unnerving side, but a memorable part of our summer vacation, none the less."

"True. OK, we won't have to ride the Silverton/Durango Train or visit the Indian cliff dwellings at Mesa Verde, since we did those things last year, unless that is, you want to, Doe."

"No, that's fine. They were enjoyable side trips, but we weren't able to keep Oro with us. We should plan things that we can all experience together?"

"Why thank you, Lea, for being thoughtful enough to include me. I've come to the conclusion that businesses don't like animals."

"I don't believe it's that, Oro. It's usually a liability issue."

"OK, gang, let me run some ideas past you that I picked out from the tour book. We drive to Montrose for our first night and travel from there to Olathe to take in the fun at their annual Corn Festival."

"Will, ears of corn from Olathe are known far and wide as some of the best corn in the country."

"That's true. The festival will begin in two days and we could visit there before heading south to Ouray. Our two overnights in Ouray would include a day trip to Telluride. We would then move on to the Durango area for another two days."

"Will we stay at the campground where you met Darcie and me?"

"That's correct. For the final leg of our plans, we might schedule an overnight at Creede and conclude the tent camping with a single night at San Cristabol Lake, south of Lake City.

"That seems an appropriate place to spend our last night out on your little safari, since the event at the lake last summer is one reason why we will be in the area again."

"Good. Now that our itinerary is fairly set, let's pack up what we have for the trip and drive into town to buy what we will need and have supper out for a change of pace."

"That sounds like a fun trip."

"Since I'm a very poor packer, I'll supervise the operation."

"Oro, that reminds me of my visit to Gander Mountain with Gary and James. I saw a saddle style, back pack for dogs. We'll have to buy one somewhere on the trip, so you can carry your own water and food when we go hiking."

"Uh oh, I should have kept my mind shut."

We had entered the outskirts of Gunnison when I stated my intentions of stopping by the post office.

"Lea, I want to introduce you to a few people there."

"Oh, I know who he's talking about," Oro said to Lea. To me he continued with, *"You want her to meet the ladies who work there. Right?"*

"That's correct."

"Well, clue me in, Dear."

"OK. Last summer, Oro and I were out killing time and we dropped by the post office to buy some stamps for post cards."

"It was while you were in town shopping and Will took me inside with him."

"Oro, do you want to tell her the story?"

"No, Boss, go ahead, but I'm right here if you need me ... or if you leave anything out."

"Thank you. Now, where was I?"

"You took Oro inside the post office."

"Yes, I did. Once inside, I noticed a large rectangular banner that read, 'Our goal is five minutes or less' and for some reason I just had to ask the clerk about its significance."

"Of course you did, Dear. It's part of your inquisitive nature."

"That's probably true and thanks for leaving the fact that I'm nosey out of the equation. So I asked for a book of post card stamps and pondered the stated goal. Maybe the post office was being criticized for being slow. She ..."

"Her name was Jodi; the one who waited on you."

"I believe you're right, Oro. Anyway, she handed me the stamps, my change and a receipt."

"Jodi also said, 'What a beautiful dog you have.'"

"Yes, she did. I see now, why you remembered her name. I told her, as I pointed to the banner, that I had four more minutes to spend at the counter, because she was so fast. She replied that the intention of the goal was that no customer would have to wait in line for service for more than five minutes."

"That sounds logical, Dear."

"It does now, but at the time I was thinking about the length of time to take care of a customer. Since there was no line at all while I was there, waiting for service didn't register."

"Don't forget about Brenda, the clerk at the other counter. She called to the back for Loretta and Cheryl to come up to see me."

"You remember their names, too? I am impressed, especially since I'm so terrible in that area. At any rate, I spoke to all of them for several minutes about Gunnison. They told me where the best places to shop and eat were and the location of the town's newspaper office, where I planned to visit to see about the syndication of my column."

"And why, if I may interrupt, do you want me to meet them?" At that moment, we arrived at the post office. I pulled into a spot and continued my story.

"You don't have to meet them, Doe. That's your choice, but I'm going in to say 'Hi' because I enjoyed visiting with them last summer. In fact, I wrote a piece about some of our vacation experiences in the area for a column back home. I sent a copy of it back to the ladies and to the paper, but the editor never ran it."

"Will, do you really expect them to remember you? They've seen thousands of vacationers since you were here."

"Don't you think I'm memorable?"

"Of course, Dear, but don't take it personal, like you did last year at the Lake City Bank, when the teller wasn't outwardly impressed after you deposited the one hundred grand check into your savings account."

"I wasn't depressed, just puzzled."

"Will, take me in with you again and I'll guarantee that you'll be remembered."

"No, I'm going to be fair about it. OK, Doe, would you like to make a small wager on whether I'll be recognized or not?"

"You know I don't bet."

"OK, never mind. Do you want to stay with Oro or come in for just a short friendly visit?"

"I'll go with you."

With Oro's help, I had recalled the names of the four women, but I couldn't remember which face went with which name.

Lea and I walked into the building and approached the left of two large service windows. I noticed the banner was no longer hanging over the counters.

I recognized the clerk ("Jodi" was imprinted on her name tag) as she spoke. "What can I do for you this morning?"

I stood there for a moment sporting a fox-in-the-chicken-coop smile on my unshaven mug.

Jodi's initial courteous, business-like smile began to expand into a more pronounced display of cheerfulness and/or amusement.

"Hey, aren't you the writer from Kansas?"

"Yes I am and ..."

Before I could finish my intended thought, she turned to the back and yelled, "Girls, get up here ... you'll never guess who's here."

What followed was a mini-reunion scene, like when you run into a family on the street, who you haven't seen for quite some time. They told Lea how funny I was, but she wasn't that impressed. The crew asked where Oro was and I was directed to bring him inside. I did and before we left the happy group of postal workers, Jodi came out into the lobby and handed me the banner that had led to our friendly bonding during my previous visits last summer.

"We were cleaning up here and were told to get rid of it, but we thought of you and decided to hold onto it and give it to you if you came by on vacation this year."

After we left and continued our trip to Wal-Mart I had to say it, "They remembered me."

Our week-long trip concluded on schedule at San Cristabol Lake. We stayed at a small, but pleasant RV stop that was within a mile of the lake and prepared for the visit to Lake City on the following morning.

CHAPTER 19

LAKE CITY

OUR WEEK-LONG, fun-filled, sightseeing trip was near an end. We had made it to San Cristabol Lake on the eve of our appointment in Lake City.

The time of the luncheon, where Oro was to be recognized for saving the young boy last summer, was set for noon-thirty. The honoree and his chaperones arrived in town early to allow the party of three (mostly Lea) ample shopping time prior to the event.

The sun had not totally thawed the chill of the morning, due to a persistent layer of clouds overhead. Lea was forced to wear sweat pants and shirt over her cute patriotic outfit that consisted of a red, white and blue v-necked pullover with white Capri's and sandals. Of course Lea looked good in anything she wore ... even when she dressed down on a cleaning day back home with mismatched old clothes.

I parked across from the Lake City Bank, at 231 Silver Street, which was centrally located in the area of tourist-oriented shops and other businesses.

"Lea, why don't you focus your efforts in the blocks north of here. I'll stay with Oro and hang out around the bank while you do your thing. I will tag along with you for the shopping assault on the southern half of the town."

"That works for me, Dear. There should be plenty of time to get some serious bargain hunting accomplished. You boys stay out of trouble and I will see you later."

Oro and I countered with our own see-ya-laters and took up temporary residence on a park bench in front of the bank.

"Oro, did you know I have an account at this bank?"

"Yes, I remember and Lea mentioned it last week how your feelings were hurt because they didn't treat you like royalty."

"Oh, I think that's stretching it quite a bit and I ..."

"In fact," Oro broke in, but I cut him off.

"OK, maybe I was a little put off. At any rate, I'm going in to check on the account's balance, just to see how much interest a hundred grand has earned in a year's time."

"In other words," Oro smiled and threw out, *"you want to show off again."*

"Oro, sometimes I hate it when you read my mind ... it's not fair," I whined with a half frown/half smile on my face.

I went inside and stood in line behind two other customers, but only briefly, before a young woman approached me from the side.

"Mr. Jacobs, I would be delighted to help you over here if you'd like," she said, as she motioned her hand in the direction of a large oak desk that was obviously an antique.

I was somewhat surprised that she knew my name, but I followed along beside her and tried not to act as bewildered as I was.

After we were both seated, she said in a friendly, but professional manner, "I'm Skipper and how may I help you today?"

"What a unique name ... I just came by to check the balance on my saving's account."

"No problem, I can access the information right here," she said as she turned to the left to face her computer screen.

I held out my passbook to her, but she had shown no interest in it. Within a few moments, she handed me a timed and dated slip of paper with the balance.

"Mr. Jacobs, is there anything else we can do for you while you're here?"

"OK, first of all you can call me 'Will' and I give up ...

how did you know who I was? I have only been in the bank twice in the last five years."

"Let's just say that our goal is to get to know all of our customers ... even the ones like you who we seldom see, since you generally do all of your deposits with us through the mail."

"I was wondering. Did my healthy deposit last year raise a few eyebrows?"

"A little, in the beginning, but then the news came out about your dog saving the Rodriquez boy at the lake. You two, even in absentia, became the talk of the town and it increased after someone ran your name on the Net and word got out about your good fortune of winning the lottery. State lottery sales actually soared in the area for quite some time."

"I'll bet the bank was happy that my deposit was legit and not drug money or from some other illegal sources."

Skipper didn't comment on the legality part of my statement, but continued with, "Oh, we were happy about your luck and pleased with your decision to share some of the proceeds with us. By the way, the news bio about you stated that you are a history teacher. We are doing a reenactment play about the trial of Alfred Packer, who you may have heard about."

"Really? Yes, I'm somewhat familiar with the story."

"Our next performance will be this evening at 6 p.m. There is a flyer with details on the board by the door. I happen to play the part of Alfred Packer's lawyer. We'll put it on every Friday night during the summer as a fund raiser for the Historical Society of Lake City."

"It sounds interesting. I'll ask my wife, Lea, if we can stay longer than we planned to take it in."

"Oh, I didn't know you were married."

"I suppose those looking for news wouldn't follow my story for long. Yes, we tied the knot earlier this month and are here as part of a combination honeymoon and vacation."

"Congratulations. Did you want to designate Lea as the beneficiary or a co-owner on your account?"

"I hadn't thought about that, since she's already in my will." I paused to think it over. "Yes, let's list her as co-owner of the account."

"That's a good choice, Will, because as a co-owner she would have no tax liability in case of your demise."

"Good, there's no sense in paying any more in taxes than is necessary."

"Let me get some information from you to get the paperwork completed for both of you to sign."

I gave Skipper the info she needed and was told that it would only be a few minutes.

"I'm meeting Lea fairly soon, so we'll be back in later to sign whatever you need."

Once outside, I walked to the bench and apologized to Oro for taking so long.

"That's fine Will. I have enjoyed taking in the assorted gossip, banter and chatter from the residents and tourists, who have passed by."

"Good, do you have any interesting stories to share?"

"Not really, but you could go over to that gentleman across the street, who is standing beside the truck that looks like yours and wish him good luck in his quest to quit smoking."

"If giving him some moral support will help him quit, then it's worth the effort. Let's go interfere into another person's life."

We crossed the wide, unmarked street and approached the tall man.

"Hello, I'm Will and this is my best friend, Oro."

The guy laughed and said, "I get it ... man's best friend. Pleased ta' meet ya' both. My name's Ray."

He offered his hand, which I took and a strong handshake followed. The guy had passed one of my tests to show character in a person.

"Ray, I don't mean to butt into your life ... actually I do

mean to do just that. I want to tell you that Oro and I are behind you all the way in your desire to quit smoking."

Ray's eyes widened, but I quickly went on. "It's worth your effort to fight the addiction of those nasty, smelly and unhealthy things."

Ray stood there in silence, but was soon grinning, which eased my mind somewhat. After all, the guy was equal in size to me and he could have easily taken exception to my interference. We exchanged looks on an even level for several moments before he spoke.

"Man 'oh man. I can't imagine how you came up with that, but you're right on. I've been tryin' to quit, but thought about buyin' a pack of smokes before you walked over."

"Well, I'm glad we made it here in time to help you out. There are certainly better and healthier things to spend your money on. How long have you gone without one, Ray?"

"Today is only six days."

"Only!" I semi-shouted out. "Ray, that's great and you are so close to a full week. Get the thought out of your head and hold out for the rest of the day to complete the week. Then work on it a day at a time and before you know it, you will have two weeks under your belt. Before long, you will have so many days put together that you won't want to break the string, but it takes one step at a time to succeed."

Oro interrupted my discussion with, *"Will, from what he's thinking, it sounds like his lady friend can't stand his habit and has sworn to break up with him, if he continues."*

"Well," Ray said, "I'm glad I made it through this near break down of will power. I thank ya' for yer help."

I reached into my pocket, pulled out my "Grizzly's This 'N That" business card and handed it to him. At the same time Oro was heard from again.

"His thoughts are on the woman, Linda, and how he doesn't want to lose her."

"Ray, you call me if you ever need to talk. Once you break the desire to smoke, the better you will be. I'm sure

Linda will be supportive of your efforts too, but remember you must quit for yourself first."

With my mention of "Linda" I again got his full attention. He overcame his surprise and almost whispered, "Did she put yawl up to this and if not, how cum you know her name? I'm positive that I never told ya' her name. Come to think of it, you never told me how you knew about my problem in the first place."

"Actually, I don't know Linda at all and I'm not even from around here. To answer your questions truthfully ... it was Oro who told me. He happens to be a very incredible dog."

I glanced over at Oro and he was smiling proudly and I could tell he was chuckling to himself.

Ray laughed and said, "Man you are too much and I don't know what to think, but I'll call ya' and let ya' know how things are goin'. I guess you two are now free to go and help someone else, who may need yawl's help."

"Well said Ray, because that is basically part of what Oro and I do best."

We walked back across the street from whence we had come. I sat back down on the bench. Ray still stood where we had left him. He was watching us and I tipped my hat to him. He returned a small wave, jumped in his truck and drove off.

"Do you think he'll make it, Will?"

"I do believe he will succeed, but smoking is a very powerful habit to break and the odds are not usually favorable. Maybe if he starts to falter and thinks of our intervention today, he will get by."

Within a few minutes, Lea arrived and Oro took the lead to report our most recent involvement with Ray.

"You two should come to my classes and spread the word to a few of my students. If young people could get passed the experimentation stages of smoking they wouldn't be so likely to become smokers as adults. I do think the trend is becoming 'less cool' in school, but the problem certainly still exists."

I then told Lea of my dealings with the bank. We entered to take care of the need to sign a new signature card. I introduced her to Skipper, who again mentioned the upcoming play.

While we sat chatting at her desk, Lea noticed a large framed picture of two girls on a shelf alongside the computer.

"Skipper, I'll assume that the picture is of your girls. Are they twins?"

"No, but they were born within a year of each other and most people think they are, since they've looked so much alike ever since they were quite young. They are ten and eleven now"

I sat there, patiently, while the two exchanged words about the girls, the town and the state of educational facilities in the area.

"Lea, I think we'd better continue with the shopping, although I'm not sure we will be done before the ceremony."

"You're right Dear. Do we have enough time to go to Skipper's play this evening?"

"Even if we don't, we'll make time."

"Good, I guess we will see your performance later, then."

"Great," Skipper replied with a smile, "I do hope you enjoy it. I might be able to bring the girls too. I'm sure they would like to tell you all about their school and what they are doing."

We left the bank and I snapped Oro's leash onto his collar and started to walk south, down the sidewalk towards the first shop in the block. But Lea stood beside the passenger door and looked at me with that ever-present, loving smile of hers.

"Will, I bought you a gift. Do you want it now or later?"

"If it's not for any special occasion, then now would be fine Doe … unless you want to keep it as a surprise for a later date. I'll let you decide."

"All right, I'll give it to you now. I can never keep a surprise locked away for any length of time."

She went through her collection of sacks, pulled one aside, opened it and handed me a tissue-wrapped parcel.

"Happy Nothing-in-Particular Day, Dear."

I unfolded the wrapping and exposed a nice long sleeved sweatshirt. Centered across the front of the shirt was a line of my favorite animal ... bears, of course. Underneath them, "Lake City, Colorado" was embroidered in bold black letters.

"Thank you, Love. I really like this."

"I bought it at the Lake City Shirt Co.," she said while pointing north. "If you wish to exchange it for a different size or color ..."

I broke in with, "No, it's the right size and the light tan is a good outdoorsy color."

"Speaking of gifts," Lea added, "I have come up with a solution for when we should celebrate your birthday, Oro."

"Great," Oro returned. *"Is it today?"*

"No," she laughed, "I thought it would be unique to select August 19th as the date. Do either of you boys know why?"

Lea waited a few moments for a reply. I shrugged my shoulders and Oro, who may not have been able to shrug, simply shook his head.

"Oh my, and here I thought the date was such an obvious choice for you, Will. August 19th, if it's not a Leap Year, is the 231st day of the year."

"I can hardly believe I never figured out what day of the year coincided with my favorite number. Oro, does the date suit you?"

"I would have to say it does, because it's better than not having a day at all."

"And," Lea added, "that makes your birthday, at least for celebration purposes, only a few weeks away."

"Do you mean that I can have a party and invite Jay Jay ... and maybe some people?"

"Yes, you can, Oro. You guys can make an invitation

list shortly after we return home and I'll take care of the party end of everything."

"Thank you, Lea. I've got to be the luckiest dog around."

"Well, special treatment for a special dog seems only right."

CHAPTER 20

THE AWARDS PRESENTATION

W E COMPLETED OUR gift hunt on South Main, but postponed the shopping scheduled for the east half of town until after Oro's moment of glory. Our time management plan had briefly failed us, but it was OK. We proceeded to the courthouse early enough to meet with various town officials, the fire department's rescue squad and a host of other people I knew I would never remember. After a few introductions, the names just became a blur. Of course, Mr. Rodriquez and his son, Robert, were there, since the whole affair was arranged by the boy's father in the first place.

The presentation was void of any long speeches (there must not have been an election forthcoming), but it was sincere. A Chamber of Commerce representative placed a medallion attached to a braided gold cord over Oro's head. The inscription on the award said, "To Oro – In appreciation of your heroic actions that were instrumental in the saving of a human life." A commemorative wall plaque was also given to me for our hero, along with the ceremonial "Key to the City."

I could tell he was pleased to be recognized and that he loved the attention. Lea and I were extremely proud of him. He had certainly been deserving of praise for many of his actions in the past and now he was enjoying his time in the spotlight. Oro, as I found out later, was also part of history for the town. The annual humanitarian "Helping Others" award from the city had never been given to an animal.

A public, open-air, meet-and-greet reception was arranged for after the presentation. Oro received enough pats on the head to last him for quite some time.

Robert Rodriquez was one of the first to congratulate Oro at the reception. The boy knelt down on both knees in front of Oro and spoke to him so quietly that I could not hear what was said. He then leaned forward and gave Oro a lengthy hug and followed that up with a kiss to his forehead. As the boy rose, I saw several tears roll down both cheeks of the lad, before he could wipe them away. It was quite a touching scene.

Mr. Rodriquez came over to give his thanks to all three of us for being able to make it to the event.

"I thank God," he said, "every day for putting you two and Oro in the right place at the right time to save Robert's life. I would never have been able to rid myself of the guilt if he had perished, due to my neglect on that day."

We accepted his praise as humbly as possible and thanked him for honoring Oro.

After the reception, we (mostly Lea) returned to the shopping mode of the trip, in search of things for the house or gifts for friends back home. I relaxed in the park with Lake City's official celebrity of the day.

"Oro, if it isn't too personal, can you tell me what the boy said to you? I could tell it was certainly an emotional moment."

"I suppose his fear of dying in the lake was quite strong by the time I reached him. I recall 'speaking' out to him, like when I communicate with you, to let him know that he would be all right and I 'told' him to get on my back. Of course he grabbed for whatever he could and I had a tail ache for the rest of the week, but ..."

I unintentionally interrupted his story, for I began to laugh. "Oro, I'm not making light of what happened, but it was so funny, after the fact, when you were moaning on the side of the lake about how your tail hurt. I'm sorry, please, continue."

"Yes, I suppose it was a little humorous. At any rate, today, he told me that he had actually 'heard' me speak to him and that he was very thankful to be alive. He asked me if I was his guardian angel."

"That is amazing, Oro. It would seem that you are actually able to communicate with others in certain circumstances. Did you know he was able to hear you?"

"No, I knew nothing about it until he told me at the reception."

"Did you answer his question about being his guardian angel?"

"Yes, I did. I told him that I must have been, at that particular point in time, but I could tell that he wasn't able to hear me."

I was about to respond, but Lea suddenly came up behind us. She was carrying several small sacks and looked pleased with herself.

"Are you two tired of waiting around for me? I'm ready for a bite to eat. How does that sound? The finger foods at your banquet, Oro, weren't too filling."

"Lea, if I were by myself I might find the shop-till-you-drop time a tad bit boring, but with Oro, there's always something of interest in the air. Sit down and listen to what happened in the lake when Oro went out to save the Rodriquez boy."

Oro proceeded to recount the story to Lea that he had told me.

"That is remarkable, Oro. I can certainly understand how the boy would think of you as his guardian angel. Will, you should write a book about the exploits of Oro … you could call it 'Oro, The Incredible Dog' or something to that effect."

"Doe, it's said that great minds run along the same track. I actually have been making notes about our times with Oro and earlier today I called him 'incredible' to a complete stranger. Is that ironic or what, that you should mention that as part of a book title? Oro, why don't you tell her that tale too?"

I let him tell Lea the story for two reasons. Lea was always excited when Oro "spoke" to her and was still amazed that they could now communicate with each other and Oro loved explaining how his special ability had assisted in helping others. I was also pleased that I didn't have to keep repeating what happened or what was said with Oro.

"You guys are just, pardon the old teenage expression, 'too cool'. Oro, I must take you on a walk, so I can be directly involved in one of your episodes."

"I'm sure that can be arranged. Right, Will?"

"Certainly, but for now, let's fulfill Lea's request and find a place to eat. I remember seeing a restaurant not far from here, along the highway. Does that suit everyone?"

"If we went to the Sonic down the street we wouldn't have to leave Oro out in the Jeep."

"OK, Sonic it is then. After that, we should head back to the old courthouse. The reenactment play will be in the very courtroom where Alfred Parker was tried for murder over 100 years ago."

Lea and Oro agreed to the proposal. We decided to sit, visit and eat at Sonic's small outside picnic area. After the meal we drove to the site of the play.

"Oro, would you like to watch the play with us?"

"Yes, I would, Will, but ... "

"It just so happens that I have a little something for you that was given to be me by Captain Rigley. He said to use it with discretion."

Lea looked slightly confused, but said nothing, as I reached behind the back seat and pulled out a paper sack. I withdrew a bright yellow dog vest from the sack. "Service Dog" was imprinted on both sides of the vest.

I believe Lea and Oro both uttered, "Oh, my," simultaneously.

"Rigley told me that I would now be able to take Oro with me to investigate or do whatever it is that we do."

"Will, you should get Oro 'service dog' certified ... to make it official."

"That's a good idea, Doe."

"I'll second that motion."

The performance, which lasted less than two hours, was historically accurate, from my point of view and enjoyed by all of those in attendance … especially Oro.

After the presentation, performed by several of the town's "not ready for prime time" cast members, our family met with Skipper and her two daughters, Taylor and Tori. The females of the group sat outside on the steps of the courthouse and chatted.

I opted to take Oro on a walk for his required break time. We strolled only two short blocks to where the forest met the carved out western perimeter of the community. It was still light out, but the warmth of the sun's rays had slipped below the mountains. The cool of the evening was once again upon us.

Shortly after we returned to where we had left the girls, the decision was made to call it a day. It was time to return to our tent site at San Cristabol Lake. Tomorrow we would return to the luxury of the Eagle for a short time before heading home.

On the drive back to Blue Mesa Ranch, Lea made an observation. "Will, I know you have mentioned several times of your desire to move to Colorado. If we ever do, I'd like Lake City to be on the list of possible places. I love much of what I've seen here. Skipper even said that there are two spots in the K-12 school here that haven't been filled for the fall yet."

"For years, Lea, I've wanted to move out here and live in the mountains. I suppose I still do, but I love our home at Rainbow Acres so much … it's too bad we didn't find the same house in this area or, for that matter, anyplace throughout central Colorado."

We had completed a full week of varied activities and would have many fond memories of this particular visit to Lake City. Once back inside the Eagle, I took Oro's plaque and placed it in a prominent spot on a shelf for pictures and such. I also took his engraved medallion off its lanyard and placed it on his collar. I knew he was proud of the award for his deed, but he never "said" anything to me about it. If it had been me, I would have at least gloated a little. Yes, Oro was, without a doubt, an incredible dog.

CHAPTER 21

ORO'S BIRTHDAY BASH

O<small>N THE MORNING</small> following the return of the Eagle to its home at Rainbow Acres, every member of the Jacobs' clan slept in late. The return trip had been enjoyable until Colorado Springs was in our rear view mirror. We (mostly I) then had to face the depressing fact that we were leaving the Rockies behind once again.

When my eyes were able to focus well enough to make it out, the large-faced digital clock on the bureau across the room from our bed displayed 9:59. I could hardly believe it was that late, for Lea and I had retired shortly after watching the 10 p.m. news the night before.

Looking back though, I realized that the previous day had been a long one; without a nap, I might add. We had risen early and were on the road before seven. To make the journey a little more interesting, we took a different route home and made a southern, back-door entry into the Royal Gorge Park.

I was glad the suspension bridge was open to vehicular traffic. If it had been closed for any reason, we would have had to back track and drive at least fifty miles out of our way.

The bridge happens to be the world's highest of its kind. Lea and Oro opted to walk the open expanse of the structure that crossed the gorge. The Arkansas River flowed 1,053 feet below. In the Eagle, I could feel, as well as see the bridge sway back and forth, which was a slightly disconcerting feeling. I felt much better after I reached the parking lot on the north side.

We left Oro in the Eagle (he volunteered to stay), toured a few of the shops at the park and returned to the motor home. Before leaving the lot, we fed several deer that were wandering around looking for handouts. We did so in front of "don't feed the deer" signs, because the animals looked like they were starving. We gave them what was left of the cracked corn that had been brought along to feed the chipmunks and squirrels at Rainbow Lake.

Our last extracurricular stop on the way home was at the "Old" Colorado Springs district. I knew there was an abundance of specialty stores and shops along several blocks of the area. Lea was sure to enjoy spending an hour or so leisurely shopping prior to the ten-hour road trip ahead. Besides …

"Pardon the interruption, Will, but are you going to reminisce about the whole trip home or what?"

"Oro, why are you eavesdropping into my mind and what else do I have to do at this time?"

"You could start by feeding me for one thing and I'm sure other chores will be forthcoming as the day goes by."

Lea stirred, propped herself up on one elbow and entered the conversation.

"Good morning, boys. I heard you speaking, Dear, but not you, Oro. Don't tell me that I can't communicate with you again."

"No, everything is fine, Lea. I simply didn't direct my thought to you … a selective broadcast, so to speak."

"Thank goodness. I'd hate to go back to being left out of everything that goes on between you two."

"Now that you're awake too, will you be getting up soon? You are pretty enough, so you don't need any more beauty sleep."

"Yes, I need to get going and thank you for the kind words. Are you buttering me up for a treat?"

"Doe, I believe there's a plan going on inside that brain of his. If he were wearing a shirt, I'd have to say he has something up his sleeves, so we'd better follow along."

"Let's say that I do have an idea I want to throw on the table for both of you. I'll leave now and let you get dressed."

I was at the kitchen table reviewing the editorials in the morning paper, while Lea was in the process of cooking up a few things for breakfast. Oro was outside playing with Jay Jay, who had come over, without Kayla, for a surprise visit.

"Will, do you remember what Oro said earlier about having selective broadcasting?"

"Yes, why?"

"Do you have selective hearing?"

"I'm not following you, Doe. What do you mean?"

"Last night I asked you to take out the trash and ..."

"Oops, I'm on it, Babe."

"While you're at it, the bird feeder is empty."

I grabbed the bag from the can, inserted another liner and left through the mudroom, pausing only to grab a few dog treats and a dipper of wild bird food.

I refilled the feeder, headed for the trash dumpster and called for the dogs after depositing the bag. They were soon sitting patiently in front of me, waiting for the tasty morsels they could smell, but not see.

"OK, here ya' go," I said, as I tossed the biscuits into the waiting mouths. I envisioned myself feeding fish to killer whales at Sea World, for the experience had its similarities.

"Oro, I'm going in for chow."

"Is it all right for Jay Jay to come in with us?"

"Sure, as long as you'll share and let him lick one of the breakfast plates clean."

"No problem. He can have your plate and I'll take Lea's."

"What difference does it make?"

"You never leave anything on your plate."

"Oh, really? I'm not sure I like the implication of ..."

"Don't dwell on it, Will. Let's go!"

We did. Once inside, I topped off my coffee cup and retook my usual seat at the breakfast nook; the one facing the recently restocked bird feeder. Jay Jay made himself comfortable on Oro's pad near the pantry and Oro sat beside me.

"Thank you, Dear. The food will be ready soon."

Before I could respond, Oro cut in with, *"Lea, is it too early to talk about my birthday party?"*

"Absolutely not, Oro. Would you like to start by deciding on who you want to ask?"

"I believe that would be a good place to begin. I already have thought of who I'd like to invite, but since I can't write very well, I only have a mental list."

Lea smiled and I chuckled, as she withdrew a pad of paper and a pen from a drawer in the kitchen's large countertop island. There was even a tail wag from Jay Jay, but I don't believe he was privy to Oro's subtle humor.

"Will, you take notes, while I finish the omelets," she said as she handed me the paper and pen.

"OK, Oro. I'll assume, for starters, that you'd like James, Laura and their kids to come. Who else?"

"I'd like Darcie to come. Would that be all right?"

"Of course she can come," Lea said. "In fact, I'll call her right after brunch, to see when she's available and we can set the date to fit her schedule."

"Good idea, Doe. OK, Oro, is that all?"

"No, actually I'd also like to ask your friend Gary, Captain Rigley, Neal and Max."

"OK. I'm sure Gary would like to drop by and I had about forgotten about our K-9 friends, but I doubt that Rigley would come."

"Oh, I don't know. He has an inquisitive and interesting mind and I know he's more than a little curious about us."

"Yes, he is that, for sure. OK, if that's the group, we

will start the ball rolling by contacting Darcie first ... after breakfast, if that's OK?"

"By all means. Jay Jay and I will stay to clean plates and then go out and chase Fluffy."

Lea and I both spoke to Darcie, Oro's previous owner, on the speakerphone. She lived in Oklahoma City now and was delighted to hear from us. She thought it was a great idea that Lea had picked a day to celebrate Oro's birthday.

"When I acquired him from the local shelter, they never gave me a date of birth for him," she told us.

August 19th, the date selected for the party worked well with her schedule and she readily accepted the invitation and Lea talked her into staying over with us for two nights.

Ever since Lea learned that I had not told Darcie about Oro's gift, she had, on occasion, thrown a few old clichés in my face. I was tired of hearing, "bite the bullet and do what is right" or "be a man and step up to the plate," etc.

After the call, I told Lea I would "spill the beans" and tell Darcie how I had known of Oro's ability before accepting him from her.

All the other invitees on the short list, who could accept the invitation verbally, did so. We assumed that Jay Jay and Max would have acknowledged the request if they could. Rigley even seemed unusually pleased with being asked and I told him to bring his wife, who we hadn't met. And to rile his brain a little, I told him, "Oro thanks you for the vest and wanted to make sure you were on the list."

The birthday party went off extremely well. Oro looked the part of a king throughout the day, even without a crown, staff and throne. I was sure Rigley, whose mind was trained to think out of the box and look beyond the obvious, knew there was something special about Oro. I could see it in the Captain's eyes and mannerisms, when he looked at the dog, as if he was studying him.

It had been a pleasure meeting Rigley's better half. Barbara Rigley was a pleasant woman of about double nickels in age, I suppose. I could tell she admired her man and that the feeling was mutual, for Rigley spoke to her in an entirely different way than he did with others. With Barb, his abrasiveness and condescending manner disappeared.

Oro spent most of his time with the kids, Max and Jay Jay. After the cookout, we all had cake with ice cream and sat around on the porch to relax. The party for a marvelous animal had been a marvelous success and I believe our guests left feeling the same as I did about the event.

The time had come for me to fess up to Darcie. Originally, I had thought to talk with her before she left for home on the day after the party. I could not wait another day to get the truth out in the open. Oro sensed the change in my plans.

"Will, what you have to say may be hurtful, but things will be all right in the end. I am behind your decision and will be there to support you."

"Thank you, my friend. She may hate me after she learns what I did, but I pray that she understands in the end."

We found Lea chatting with Darcie in the kitchen. Oro and I had previously gone over what I had to do.

The girls' discussion dealt with Darcie's new job as an assistant clothes designer with a prestigious firm in Oklahoma City. It seemed like the discussion had come to a close, for they looked at me as if it was my turn to begin a new discussion. I obliged them.

"Darcie, I learned of an incredible secret within a

few minutes after I first met you and Oro back at that campground north of Durango last summer. It was not right for me to keep what I discovered from you. I learned that Oro and I have the capability to telepathically communicate with one another."

I watched Darcie's expression carefully as I began to talk to her and through my conversation with her. Her full smile in the beginning, slowly faded to a casual one, but then went full again, like when one listens to a joke being told, but they don't quite get it. She stared at me, but said nothing. It was Lea who spoke up.

"Darcie, I was not pleased with Will's decision not to tell you about what Oro can do. I was told the story after we left Durango that summer. I could have told you later, after our return, but didn't, so maybe I am to blame for this oversight as well."

"You two have me totally confused. Lea, is this a game of some kind?"

"No, Darcie, it's surreal, I know, but what Will's saying is truth."

"Darcie, stay with me on this and you'll understand, as Lea did, about what Oro can do. Oro has informed me, telepathically, about various incidents in your past, that I would have no way of knowing."

"What incidents?"

"He told me about a time when you thought your roommate was stealing money from you. This was one of the reasons why you moved out of the apartment near the OSU campus. The culprit was not Stephanie, your roommate, but Chris, her boyfriend. Oro witnessed him taking money from your purse. Of course he couldn't tell you of what he saw, because he was unable to communicate with you."

Darcie's eyes widened, as she looked at the ceiling, seemingly in a trance.

"When you signed the lease at the other apartment that didn't allow pets, you were committed to move and forced to find a new home for Oro. He was unhappy for two reasons. He didn't want you to give him away and he was afraid that you were going to let Greg, your uncle, take him. He told me that he was afraid of your uncle and didn't want to be with him."

I saw tears begin to form in Darcie's eyes as she spoke. "I didn't really want to give him away. I was sad, too."

As the shock of what I had revealed to Darcie wore off, the point of my talk to her slowly sank in. She took the news even calmer than I expected. I was afraid she would want Oro back, but the subject was never brought into the conversation. Lea and I shared stories about situations that came up because of Oro's gift and how they were handled. Darcie seemed to understand the positive role that Oro now held in life as a member of our family. She left, in good spirits, early the next morning.

CHAPTER 22

THERAPY DOG TRAINING

 EARLIER IN THE year, Lea had utilized Oro's special, if not mystical, talent to learn what the underlying problems were with a few of her students. Successful completion of that project enabled Lea to adjust her teaching methods to get them through their difficulties in school and help the youths in other ways as well.

At the time, Lea was permitted to use Oro in the classroom by her principal, but circumstances had changed. A new superintendent was brought on board at the end of the school year. He had heard that pets were allowed in classrooms for various reasons, but there was no established procedure that permitted this.

He directed the board of education to establish an official policy on the subject. The board decided that dogs and their handlers would have to be therapy dog certified before they would be allowed in any district school. A liability issue was evidently the main reason for the tougher guidelines. There were other requirements for other pets, but they didn't involve our situation.

Lea learned of the new rules concerning pets in the classroom from the school district's latest newsletter. She reviewed the changes with Oro and me.

"That's not good news. I was looking forward to helping you again this fall, if you had any students with problems like you had last year."

"I know, Oro. I suppose we'll have to find out how to get all of us certified. Right, Will?"

"Most certainly. I'll check to see what it takes to meet

the school's new requirements."

I found out where the training was provided and made an appointment to visit Happy Tail Ranch, a place that catered to dogs. The center's main business was in canine boarding and care, but they also specialized in obedience and other types of training.

I woke early, because of a light tap from a paw upon my back.

"It's barely 6:00 a.m., Oro. What's up? The dog door is open, if you need out."

"No, it's not that, Will. I wanted to know if we were still going to the dog training center today. Uh ... we are, aren't we?"

"Yes, we are, but our appointment is not until ten-thirty," I whispered. "You didn't wake Lea did you, because she enjoys sleeping in on Saturdays so much?"

"No, but I was going to next. I guess I won't, now."

"Good decision."

"So, are you going back to sleep?"

"I suppose not. Since I'm fully awake now, I might as well just get up."

In the kitchen, I put on the normal morning pot of coffee and Oro was kind enough to trot down to the end of the drive and retrieve the daily paper.

I was pleased that he was always willing to get my paper. This morning, although I wasn't upset with him, I believe he was sorry about waking me up far too early and simply wanted to make amends.

Later, at a more presentable time, Lea got up and offered to fix me an omelet for breakfast. I quickly accepted, of course and while she prepared the meal, we discussed the plans for the short day trip to rural Valley Center, a few miles north of Wichita.

At Happy Tail Ranch we met Janice, the certified trainer. She gave us a tour of the center's facilities and explained a lot about the program.

"If there is anything that I left out, it will be in one of these brochures about what is required to enter the program and become certified as a handler and dog team," she said, as she handed Lea some printed materials. The time spent there was short, but productive.

During the drive home, little was said, for we all seemed to be digesting what the trip had meant to each of us in different ways.

Once home, Lea told us not to get involved with anything too time consuming, because she was going to fix us lunch. Oro and I departed the kitchen for the study, where I began looking over the information about the therapy dog training.

"Let's see, Oro, I mentioned the part about needing to take you to the vet for an appointment, but it's more involved than just having a check up. You'll need a dental check, a blood check for heartworm, a fecal check and ..."

"Sounds like you had better bring your 'check' book. Do you get it?"

"Yes, I do. You're a funny boy now, but you might want to reconsider when you hear about all the shots that are required. There are shots for parvo, distemper and influenza. A rabies vaccination is also mandatory, which you are current on, but here's something about being checked for kennel cough, which I'm clueless about."

"I'm ready for whatever it takes to begin the training. Who said, 'No pain, no gain?'"

"OK, boy. Better thee, than me, because I hate shots. I can't even watch someone getting a shot on TV, much less in person. Taking you in for shots may be harder on me than you, so I might get Lea to do it."

"What a wimp you are, but that's all right. We can't all be perfect."

"That's true, Oro. At any rate, I'll schedule an

appointment for you with the vet and register all of us for the next therapy dog training class."

"Great! From what Janice said earlier, I think the sessions will be fun. Oh, and I was only kidding when I called you a wimp."

"I know, Oro, but in a way, I suppose I am."

Oro was outwardly excited, even before we entered the fair sized metal building. It would serve as our classroom for a few evenings of practice sessions, prior to the big test at the end of the week.

We arrived at the same time as several other owners and their dogs, so check in seemed to drag on for a longer period than it actually was.

"OK, gang, let's get started," shouted Janice to the class. The group had been mingling around the large meeting room for some time, waiting, as we had, for everyone to sign in for the training.

Our instructor, in another attempt to quiet the crowd, spoke again with her outside voice. "We need to begin, so you can get out of here on time."

Only half of the warm-blooded bodies assembled were paying any attention to what she was saying. A few of the trainees were yapping while some had even decided to lie down on the floor to wait for something to happen.

After order had been restored, Janice spoke again. "Let's start by introducing yourself and your partner to the group and why you are here. She pointed towards the lady beside us in a non-verbal command for her to start.

"I'm Terry and this," as she pointed to her companion, who occupied her lap, "is Tucker." Terry spoke some about why she wanted Tucker to be certified. She wished to have him at work with her as an incentive for kids to come to the library, where she was employed. Once done speaking, Terry looked over to me to indicate that I was next.

I obliged her with, "Hello, I'm Will, aka, Grizzly and this is Oro, aka, The Incredible Dog."

My introduction brought about a few laughs from some of those in attendance, but not one bark came from the twenty-odd canines present. This was a good thing, because barking, I learned from the introductory brochure, is one trait that could boot a four-legged applicant out of the class. Come to think of it, barking by a dog's master might exclude them, too.

The evening was the first of three training sessions to be followed by a night of testing. Successful completion of the process would certify those attending as a Therapy Dog & Handler Team.

"So, what type of dogs are allowed to be therapy dogs?" you might ask. Well, let me tell you, for I've done the research. Dogs must be at least a year old, but there are no stipulations as to a particular breed; pure and mixed breeds are accepted for the training. Whether or not they pass is another story.

Oro's class consisted of dogs of all sizes and included Terry's terrier, a schih Tzu, a cocker spaniel, an American bulldog, a poodle mix, a shepard/lab mix, a collie, a sheltie, three golden retrievers, a sheepdog and an assortment of others. Most of the dogs in the class were larger breeds, like Oro, who stood above the rest of the class, literally, due to his part great Dane ancestry.

After a half hour or so of introductions, we were allowed to go outside for a short potty break (for the dogs, of course). Oro informed me that he was good, so we walked over to chat with Janice.

"Is it possible for the dog to pass and the handler flunk?" I asked her.

"Certainly," she informed me. "I won't pass a handler if they are abusive in their manners or actions towards any dog and I've disqualified a few people because it appeared that they were not taking proper care of their animal."

"That's interesting," I said while she beckoned to the group to say that the break was over.

Oro interjected with, *"Will, even if you flunk the test, I'll let you take me around to places."*

"Thanks, Oro, that's comforting to know."

We would soon learn that the training of the dog and owner is more accurately an evaluation of how the team (mostly the dog) reacts to various situations. My favorite scenario involved Janice along with her assistants, Karol and Cathy, in a meet-and-greet session with a twist. The three had taken on the role of being handicapped in one way or another. A wheel chair, a walker and a cane were used as props. Each handler/dog pair was directed to roam in and around the evaluators and paws, oops, I mean pause, in the middle of the three. The team was required to remain calm during this period of time while Janice and company closed in to pet the dog on one end and possibly grab a tail (the dog's tail) at the other end.

Another "test" involved walking the dog alongside food (a dog biscuit) placed in the pathway. Neither the dog, nor his master, is allowed to make a lunge for the food. If the treat had been a cheeseburger, I believe I would have failed that portion of the trials, for I could have used a snack.

A handler whose dog jumps up on people, is aggressive to other dogs or even barks too much (an objective call) will find his or her duo out of the program.

There were a number of other small, easy to pass tasks that each dog and owner were required to complete, but it was time consuming for all twenty-three teams (the final count of those participating) to get through and end the first evening.

As the certified title indicates, a dog's mere presence has a therapeutic value to kids with special needs in schools and patients, both young and old, in hospitals.

Their greatest use, however, probably occurs in nursing and care homes across the country. In most situations, since the residents are not permitted to have pets, the elderly at these facilities have often lost out on a most important part of their lives. The rewards, we were told, that a handler receives are from the smiles they bring to the faces of those they meet.

The other two evening sessions were optional. If a handler was confident that his/her dog would pass, they could opt out of the practices and return for the actual test/evaluation. As we drove away from Happy Tail Ranch, I queried Oro.

"Well, what did you think of the experience?"

"I thoroughly enjoyed myself and look forward to the next session. It was fun to be out mingling with others ... both your kind and mine. So, what's your opinion of the class?"

"I enjoyed myself, too and from what I saw, most of the teams present will have no trouble passing the course. As for the next session ... I know we will do fine on the evaluation this Friday, so we could skip the other practices?"

"Oh, I'm certain we will pass, but I'd like to learn more about some of those who were there tonight."

"Oro, are you saying there are some sub-plots to the story? What gives, boy?"

"I did pick up some information that I'd like to follow up on, so could we at least go back Wednesday evening?"

"OK, that's no problem, but would you like to clue me in? We are partners, don't ya' know?"

"That's true, but I didn't want to set off any alarms until I knew more. First off, Brandon, the guy with the collie, is saddened by the fact that his dog, Sadie, will probably not live out the year. It has something to do with the results from the vet exam done on his dog for the class."

"I see. I'll bring up the subject with him tomorrow evening. Anything else?"

"I do know that Terry, the woman who was beside us with Tucker, is quite concerned that her dog will fail part of the test Friday."

"I did notice how her pooch was not doing well in obeying a few of the required commands. I don't know that we can do anything about her situation."

"Probably not, but I'd like to experiment with a few ideas I've had lately."

"Hey, that sounds like an interesting topic. Would you care to run anything by me?"

"Oh, I've tried to communicate with other animals as I do with you and Lea. It has worked on a few occasions, but only to a limited degree. Next time, we need to be near Tucker to see if I can establish a viable contact with him."

"Sounds spooky, Oro ... like a séance or something along those lines. Before you know it, you'll be out conjuring up spirits from the past."

"Now that's a thought."

Back at home, Oro and I brought Lea up to speed on what we did at the training session. Lea listened, with keen interest, to my version of the past few hours, which, I might add, was frequently edited by Oro.

"Oro, I do look forward to my practice with you on Thursday night."

"Me too and I know you'll have a good time."

The training on Wednesday ran smoother than Monday's, since most of those present had already enrolled and knew the drill. There were a few new faces and a few who weren't there from before, so the total numbers stayed about the same.

We positioned ourselves near Terry and Tucker. I never "heard" of any communication between Oro and the terrier, but I could tell from Oro's attitude that something was going on.

At the break, I neared Brandon and talked about the vet services required for the program. After a few minutes of prodding, I decided to give up on being a part-time investigative reporter. Then, seemingly from nowhere, Brandon blurted out a statement.

"Sadie's been diagnosed with a brain tumor and her prognosis is bleak for any long term survival."

"Oh, my, I'm sorry to hear that. So they can't operate to remove it?"

"They could, but I can't afford the surgery."

"Say, why don't you give me your number. I'm sure our vet runs an internship program with vet students from the college and performs some fairly major procedures as a training op for them, which substantially reduces the cost to the animal owner. It's like what Kansas State does in their vet program up in Manhattan for horses."

"I could only afford 'free', but here's my card, anyway," he said, as Janice's outside voice was heard once again to bring us back together.

The rest of the evening progressed just as Monday's training had and we were done on time.

Thursday arrived and I tagged along with Lea and Oro for her only practice session. I watched, as they performed flawlessly through all phases of the program. Now we were all ready for the final evaluations on the following night.

Earlier in the day, I had spoken to our vet concerning the problem with Sadie. I found that I was correct about his clinic being a teaching animal hospital and he told me to have the dog's owner call for an appointment, "as *soon* as possible." His added emphasis on "soon" prompted me to call the number on the card I had been given and I relayed the Doc's message to Brandon.

At the first break during the evening's practice, while Lea and Oro were outside, he came over and actually had a smile on his face.

"Will, thanks for checking into things for me with your vet. Sadie and I are going in tomorrow morning to get her reexamined. I'll let you know if I find out news of anything before the test."

"Great! I hope you'll have only good news to share."

The long awaited test night arrived for man, woman and beast. There were two teams scheduled to participate that we had never seen at any of the practices earlier in the week. I learned that the two dogs had not passed the last scheduled test. Their owners were giving it another shot. One of the newcomers lowered Oro into second place, as far as being the largest dog in the class. Brutus (aptly named) was an English mastiff, who weighed at least fifty pounds more and stood a good four inches taller than Oro, whose eyes widened, as the strange one lumbered into the building, but he made no mention of the giant.

The testing requirements for each team proceeded in the precise order that we had practiced the procedures, so there were no surprises. The group did quite well, except for Brutus.

In a meet-and-greet scenario with a stranger (not described before), he confronted and growled at the dog on the team, who had approached them. Even though the mastiff did not strike, offensive behavior was not allowed. The young gal in charge of him was totally disgusted, which was understandable, because her dog would certainly not pass.

Since Lea and I both wanted to be certified handlers, we switched back and forth with Oro to complete what was required and passed, of course, with flying colors.

Lea and I watched, as Terry put Tucker through the phase that had been such a problem for the dog previously. He followed her commands to "sit," "lay down" and "stay," obediently, which was something he had never fully accomplished before in practice. Terry was beaming with delight and looked around, almost in shock or at least disbelief, over her dog's performance. I flashed a thumbs-up sign to her and she lipped a "Thank you," across to us.

At the end of the evaluations, we learned that all teams, but one, had passed and Janice was kind enough not to embarrass the owner by mentioning which team failed, but it was obvious to those in the group.

Right before we left the building, a smiling and composed Brandon came up to us with Sadie. I introduced him to Lea, since they hadn't met before and he reported on his vet visit from earlier in the day.

"Will, I want to again thank you so much for involving yourself with my situation. Your vet viewed the various x-rays of Sadie that I had brought with me and confirmed the fact that she does have a brain tumor."

"Oh, I'm sorry," Lea said softly. "Will told me about it earlier. Can anything be done?"

"Well, the vet told me about a fund that was already in place to help pet owners pay for services if they were in need. After a short interview with me, he said that I would qualify for assistance and there would be no cost to me for the operation on Sadie."

Lea, Oro and I simultaneously made comments ranging from, "All right!" to "That's great!"

"I couldn't believe it, myself," he went on. "If I hadn't talked with you about her problem, she probably would be dead in a few months. When I asked the vet about the fund, he said it had recently been set up by an anonymous donor. What a coincidence is that? I take her in on Monday for the operation."

"We all wish her the best, Brandon," Lea offered. "You'll need to keep us posted on how she is doing."

On the way home, I confessed to my companions who the "anonymous donor" was, but I wasn't fooling anyone, for Lea and Oro already knew.

"Will, it's fantastic how you go out of your way to do nice things for others. You are a kind and generous man."

"*My sentiments exactly, Lea. Will you are indeed a good person.*"

"Well, if I hadn't won the lottery, I couldn't have helped him. On another note … did you notice how well Tucker did? Was it luck, Oro, or did you have something to do with it?"

"*I guess I was able to finally get through to him. I told him that Terry was going to take him back to the dog pound if he didn't start doing what she asked.*"

"There's a moral to that story, boys, but I won't go there … for now. Let's go celebrate our success tonight and get an ice cream cone at Dairy Queen."

"OK, Doe. Whatever you say, Doe."

CHAPTER 23

A LOOK BACK

THE YEAR HAD been an interesting one, to say the least. Oro's ability to tie into the psyche of others was, in a way, a form of snooping into an individual's private business, but good things had come of it. Bad deeds had been punished and wrongs had been righted (Lea, is that proper English?).

Ira Fink (Lost Child) was not charged in the case and was given full custody of Marie. He filed for and obtained a divorce from his wife, Ima, who was found guilty of filing a false police report in the incident regarding her child and served thirty days in county lock-up. She was also required to serve 1,000 hours of community service, which, in the words of the judge, "doesn't begin to pay back those who went out of their way to help you."

Lea mentioned to me that she checked to see how Leslie, Jason and Gina (Making the Grade) were doing in their studies at school, since Oro had made her aware of the problems they were having.

Leslie's grades were still below average and likely to remain so until her parents took more control over the girl. Gina must have gotten her wish, for Lea learned that her father was allowed full custody and she had changed schools.

The change in Jason's diet and his workouts at the fitness center had brought about a huge transformation in his appearance and self esteem. The gift card "Santa" sent him from a clothing store didn't hurt either. His improved grades at the end of his freshman year moved him into the honor role and as a sophomore he was selected class president.

Mike Morgan (Accident or Murder?) was found guilty in a jury trial for 1st degree murder in the death of his father. He was sentenced to life in prison, without the possibility of parole. Many citizens felt that the death penalty should have been awarded. Some award, eh?

   There was strong circumstantial evidence that he had tried to do away with his sister too, but no charges were brought forth in that matter.

I received a card from Claudia (A Request from Rigley) apologizing for taking several months to thank me for helping her when she ran out of gas. She told me she had passed on the good deed she received from me, by signing Brittany up in a magnet literary middle school. She had a feeling that I had, in some way, compelled her to do this. She promised to let Brit call me in the future to set up a time for me to critique her writing.

In September, Matt Wilson (The Cookout) enrolled as a full-time student at Butler County Community College, to pursue his wish to become a CPA. His attitude and outlook improved and he established a positive rapport with his father. Matt continued to live at home and agreed to help his father on the farm when his studies allowed.

We never heard anything from or about Tony and Sam (K-9 Training), but that was no surprise. Oro, who is the night owl of the family, watches the late CNN news and swears that he saw them on a video report from Baghdad, Iraq. The segment was about bomb sniffing dogs in the war torn city. I was never able to substantiate Oro's claim.

In August, I received a call from Ray, the guy Oro and I met in Lake City, who was trying to quit smoking. He needed and received some verbal support for obvious reasons – to keep from breaking his no smoking streak.

A Christmas card from him reported that he was still smokeless after 160 days and that Linda had agreed to be his bride next July on the first anniversary date of his quitting.

Terry Barnes' status (Therapy Dog School), at the rural library where she worked, elevated after she brought her little Tucker on scene. She launched a new reading skills promotion for elementary and middle school kids in her school district. She named it, "Partner up and Read with Your Pet."

Registration in the program, which used Tucker as its mascot and model to go by, increased the visitation of youngsters to the library threefold. More parents came on board, too. They became involved with the functions of the library and many of them trained to serve as reading tutors.

Schools in the area noted a sharp increase in the reading test levels among their students and within a short time Terry was promoted to the position of Head Librarian.

Brandon Painter (Therapy Dog School) called a few days after Sadie's brain surgery. There had been no complications in the operation and his dog was as active as before. The only side effect seemed to be that Sadie couldn't understand why she was bald.

We learned from Janice, in a Happy Tail Ranch newsletter, that Brutus was allowed to try the meet-and-greet portion of the test again and did fine. A list of nursing and care homes of who would welcome visits by therapy dog teams was included in the letter. Oro told us to sign him up, so we will soon explore that avenue for more "tails" in the future.

Our family's close relationship with James, Matt and Kayla

Wilson (Oro Makes a Friend) continued as their family grew. James married Laura in early December. We sprang to have the reception at our place as our wedding gift to them. The couple's kids would finally have a brother and sister to share their lives with.

Laura's Clean Queens business was doing so well, she now managed two full time crews, but she continued to personally come to Rainbow Acres to clean for us, with the help of Lacy and Kayla. I also made sure I always had some sort of work for Lex to do and he still called me Mr. D.

I often called on James for assistance too, especially for his skills in welding for various outside projects at our place. He always volunteered to help for free, but you know me ... I wouldn't hear of it. I'm certain the extra cash he earned for his work was appreciated.

Right before the end of the year, Oro attended service dog training, was evaluated and passed. By law, he would basically be authorized to accompany me into any business or government establishment that was open to the public at large. I did not intend to abuse the privilege of having Oro be with me, but it was great to have the option available and it did open up new opportunities to help others in the forthcoming sequel, *Oro: Canine Versus Crime.*

Printed in the United States
200640BV00003B/223-324/A

9 781595 941756